TIC-TAC-TERROR

THE HARDY BOYS ® MYSTERY STORIES

TIC-TAC-TERROR

Franklin W. Dixon

Illustrated by Leslie Morrill

WANDERER BOOKS

Published by Simon & Schuster, New York

Published by WANDERER BOOKS
A Simon & Schuster Division of
Gulf & Western Corporation
Simon & Schuster Building
1230 Avenue of the Americas
New York, New York 10020

Manufactured in the United States of America
10   9   8   7   6   5   4   3   2   1

THE HARDY BOYS is a trademark of Stratemeyer Syndicate,
registered in the United States Patent and Trademark Office

WANDERER and colophon are trademarks of Simon & Schuster

Library of Congress Cataloging in Publication Data
Dixon, Franklin W.
Tic-tac-terror.
(The Hardy boys mystery stories; 74)
Summary: The two young detectives solve a mystery involving
a top secret government agency and a world-famous spy who
wishes to defect to America.
[1. Mystery and detective stories. 2. Spies—Fiction]
I. Morrill, Leslie, ill. II. Title. III. Series: Dixon, Franklin W.
Hardy boys mystery stories; 74.
PZ.D644Ti   [Fic]   81–19749
ISBN 0–671–42356–8   AACR2
ISBN 0–671–42357–6 (pbk.)

Contents

1 A Face at the Window

"Still no word from your dad!" Private detective Sam Radley's voice came crackling over the radio speaker as Frank and Joe Hardy listened tensely. "I've been waiting here in Caracas for forty-eight hours, but he hasn't contacted me."

The famous investigator, Fenton Hardy, had recently gone to South America on a top-secret mission for a U. S. Government agency. Later, he had sent for his trusted operative, Sam Radley, to join him in Caracas, Venezuela. But now it appeared that something was wrong.

"Have you tried broadcasting his emergency call signal?" asked Frank, a dark-haired senior at Bayport High.

"Half-a-dozen times, and I get no response!"

"Dad may have a reason for maintaining radio silence," put in blond, seventeen-year-old Joe, taking the microphone for a moment from his older brother. "He must be lying low."

"Let's hope that's the answer," Radley responded, though he sounded anything but sure. "I'll tell you the truth, boys. I'm getting mighty worried!"

"So are we, Sam, but there's no sense hitting the panic button too soon," said Frank. "At least hang on for a couple more days, and we'll keep our fingers crossed. Dad's been through plenty of tight spots before."

"You can say that again!" Sam agreed with a wry chuckle. "Okay, I'll wait."

As the transmission ended, Frank switched off their powerful radio transceiver with a glum sigh, then glanced at his watch and whistled. "Hey, it's almost eleven! We'd better hustle if we're going to keep that beach date!"

"You're right," Joe agreed. "But I sure don't feel in the mood for a picnic after getting that news about Dad."

"Neither do I, but the girls are expecting us and so's Biff."

The Hardys' radio shack was set up in a corner of their laboratory, which was located over the garage. The boys hurried back to the house and changed into swimming trunks, T-shirts, and rubber sandals. By unspoken agreement, they said nothing about Sam Radley's call to either their mother or Aunt Gertrude. There was no need yet to worry them about their father's safety.

As they came downstairs again, the telephone rang in the front hall. Joe answered and heard a woman's voice say, "This is Mrs. Orva Danner calling. Are you one of the Hardy boys?"

"Yes, ma'am," he said. "I'm Joe Hardy. Can I help you?"

"Oh, I certainly hope so! My brother has disappeared under very alarming circumstances, and I'm terribly worried. I'd like you and your brother to investigate it. Look, I'm calling from Axton, which isn't very far from Bayport, as you know. Could I see you if I come over right away?"

Joe hesitated and glanced at his brother. "Well, actually, Frank and I were just going out. We've been invited to a picnic at Bayview Beach, and some other people are expect—"

Mrs. Danner broke in anxiously, "Of course, I understand! What about later, then? If you're going to have lunch at Bayview Beach, perhaps we could make an appointment for sometime this afternoon?"

"Sure thing, Mrs. Danner. How about three-thirty?" Joe asked.

"That would be fine. I really appreciate any help

you can give me. I've been so worried that I hardly know what I'm do—" The voice of the caller suddenly changed to a high-pitched scream, and an instant later Joe heard the receiver come crashing down at the other end of the line.

Frank saw the startled look on his brother's face and asked, "Something wrong?"

"It sure sounded like it!" Joe hastily related the conversation and told how it had ended. "The trouble is, she didn't give me her phone number or address, so I don't even know how to check up and see if she's all right."

"You said her name was Danner?"

"Yes, Mrs. Orva Danner. She said she was calling from Axton."

"Maybe information can help us." Frank took the phone and dialed the number for directory assistance, only to be told that no one named Danner was listed in Axton or any of the other communities in the county. There was a troubled frown on his face as he hung up the receiver and ran his fingers through his dark hair. "It looks like we're out of luck, Joe," he muttered.

The telephone rang, and Frank snatched it up eagerly. "Hello?"

"Is this Joe Hardy?" asked a woman's voice.

"No, I'm his brother Frank."

"Oh—well, this is Mrs. Orva Danner. Perhaps he told you about my call a few seconds ago?"

"Yes, ma'am, he did. We were worried. Joe said he heard you scream, and then the receiver fell down."

"Yes, it was silly of me, and I'm calling back to apologize." The woman sounded embarrassed. "I guess my nerves are all unstrung. I hardly got any sleep last night, waiting up for my brother and worrying about him. What happened just now was that I glanced away from the phone and saw this face peering in through my window."

"You mean a total stranger?"

"Yes, someone I'd never seen before—quite sinister-looking with a big, drooping mustache. I was startled out of my wits! But he turned out to be just a window-cleaner."

"Are you sure?" Frank asked sharply.

"Oh yes. When I calmed down, I discovered that he was on a ladder and had a bucket of water and cleaning tools. I live in an apartment building, you see, and I just didn't know that any window-washing was to be done today."

Frank, who had been taught by his detective father to take nothing for granted, felt that the situation still sounded somewhat suspicious. "Just to play safe, Mrs. Danner," he suggested, "would you

11

mind double-checking to make sure that man was really a window-washer?"

"Well . . . no, of course not, if you think it's important." Mrs. Danner asked Frank to hold the phone.

When she came back on the line a few moments later, she sounded surprised. "How very odd! He was getting into his van just as I looked out the window, and then he went speeding off. It all happened so fast, I didn't even see the name on the van."

"Well, don't worry about it, Mrs. Danner. We'll expect to see you this afternoon, then."

As Frank hung up the phone, Aunt Gertrude came into the front hall, carrying a big picnic basket. A tall, bony woman with gold-rimmed spectacles, Miss Hardy tried to hide her fondness for her two nephews under a tart-tongued, bossy manner. "Who were those calls for?" she demanded suspiciously.

"Us, Aunty," said Joe, with a twinkle in his eye, knowing the abrupt answer would pique her curiosity unbearably.

"Another mystery case?"

"Yes." Joe was definitely teasing her now. In spite of the fact that she scolded her brother Fenton and her nephews about the dangers of detective work, both boys knew that mysteries fascinated her, and nothing gave her a greater thrill than a chance to join in their sleuthing.

"Hmph." Miss Hardy glared at the two youths through her spectacles. "And what if your caller phones back while you're gone? What should I tell him . . . or her?"

"Don't worry, Aunty," Joe said, smothering a chuckle. "She's coming here at three-thirty to discuss the case."

"Her name's Mrs. Orva Danner," Frank explained, thinking the joke had gone far enough. "It seems her brother has disappeared, but we don't have any details yet. There was a little excitement just now because she saw someone peering in the window at her—that's why she called back—but apparently it was just a window-washer."

"Window-washer, indeed!" Gertrude Hardy sniffed scornfully. "If she assumes that, the woman's a fool! The fellow might've been a crook—maybe even one of her brother's kidnappers just sizing up the situation to see how rich she is and how much ransom they could demand!"

"You're right, Aunt Gertrude. Mrs. Danner lives in an apartment building, so she didn't hire him herself. I told her to check him out, but he was gone before she had a chance," Frank explained.

13

"Hmph. Well, live and learn is what I say. Anyway, here's the picnic lunch I've packed for you. Ham and chicken sandwiches, hard-boiled eggs, and chocolate cake."

"It sure sounds like a feast!" Joe said, giving her a hug. "You're wonderful, Aunty! We'll tell you all about Mrs. Danner's vanished brother when we get the story from her."

"See that you do. I might be able to offer a few suggestions on how to find him."

"I'll bet! And good ones, too!"

The Hardys backed their yellow sports sedan out of the driveway and went to pick up their girlfriends before starting for the beach. On the way, they discussed Mrs. Danner's call.

Frank and Joe were used to having such problems brought to them. The two young sleuths had inherited a knack for solving mysteries from their father, a former ace detective with the New York City Police Department. Since retiring from the force, Fenton Hardy had become a world-famous private investigator, and his sons had cracked many cases of their own.

Stopping first at a farm just outside of Bayport, where their friend Chet Morton lived, the Hardys picked up his cute, dark-haired sister Iola, then veered back toward the bay again to get blond, brown-eyed Callie Shaw.

"Where's Chet today?" Callie asked Iola as Frank drove on Shore Road, heading for the beach.

"Oh, he's off on another one of his get-rich-quick schemes."

"Oh, no! What is it this time?" Callie asked.

"Raising white mice and rabbits. He thinks he can sell the rabbits to meat markets and the mice to laboratories for medical experiments."

"It sounds like our boy Chet all right." Joe grinned.

Iola giggled. "The trouble is he can't bear to think of anyone eating his rabbits, so he keeps making up excuses not to sell them. He's not finding too many buyers for his mice, either."

"I think I foresee a slight cage problem," Frank said.

Biff Hooper, a tall, rangy tackle on the Bayport High football team, was waiting for them at Bayview Beach with his girlfriend Karen Hunt. Biff had organized the picnic mostly to show off his new dune buggy, which he had built by hand from a salvaged hotrod chassis, a rebuilt engine, and a bright orange, fiberglass body shell.

"Biff, this is terrific!" Joe exclaimed, after he and Frank had taken turns test-driving the car up and down the sand dunes bordering the beach.

"Not bad if I do say so myself," Biff agreed, looking over his handiwork proudly. "In fact, I've got orders to make two more, if I want to go into business."

Meanwhile, the Hardys learned that Biff had landed a new afternoon job for the summer—delivering grocery orders for a supermarket.

Joe had brought along his camera. He began snapping pictures of the picnickers as they posed in Biff's dune buggy or played games on the beach, and soon shot an entire roll of film. Afterward, the group swam long enough to work up hearty appetites, then pitched into their combined feast.

"What a spread!" Frank gloated, as he and Biff finished off the remains of the chocolate cake.

Joe was already dozing in a happy glow from the warm sun and sand, the fresh sea air, and the effect of a full stomach on top of vigorous exercise. But he awakened with a start as Iola tickled the soles of his feet with a stalk of dune grass.

"Hey, cut that out!" he blurted.

"Try and make me!" She gave his feet a final tickle, then dashed into the water and stroked far out from shore.

Suddenly, she screamed and disappeared from view!

"What happened to her?" Callie exclaimed.

"Aw, she's just teasing me again," Joe said lazily.

But an instant later, the Hardys and their friends

16

saw her reappear for a moment. She was struggling wildly and screaming for help before going under again!

"Teasing, my foot! She's in trouble!" Frank cried. All three boys raced into the water to her rescue!

2 *Undersea Sneak*

The lifeguard had been off his chair for a few moments, so he had failed to react promptly to Iola's frightened cries. After seeing the three boys rushing to save her and hearing the excited exclamations from other bathers, he, too, joined in the rescue.

Luckily, Iola surfaced again, enabling them to head straight toward her. She was coughing and choking, flailing the air with both hands as she fought to keep her head above water.

Joe reached her first and supported her with one arm. The others quickly arrived at her side and helped Joe carry her to shore, where they laid her gently on the sand. After spewing up a mouthful of sea water, Iola had recovered enough to talk.

"Are you all right?" Callie asked anxiously.

Iola nodded, still catching her breath, "Y-Yes."

"Maybe we should get her to a doctor," Joe suggested to his older brother and the lifeguard.

"No, honestly . . . I'm okay now," Iola assured him.

"What happened? Did you get leg cramps?" Joe asked.

"No—someone pulled me under!"

"*What!*" There was an outburst of startled exclamations from the people hovering over her.

"You mean, someone did it just for a joke?" Frank asked in angry surprise.

Iola shook her head. "Oh, no—it was no joke. He was definitely trying to drown me—or at least scare the wits out of me!"

"Where is he? Who is this guy?" Joe exploded in a voice that promised a quick punch in the jaw to the culprit. He glared around, looking at the other bathers on the beach and in the water.

"You probably won't find him now," Iola said. "It was a frogman . . . you know, wearing scuba gear and a face mask."

"He still can't get too far away. He'll have to come ashore sometime!"

"Maybe so, but when he does come ashore, it may not be around here," Iola said.

"Why not?" Joe asked, furious but puzzled.

"Because he had one of those gadgets like a stubby little torpedo with handles on it, for scooting around underwater."

"A jet propulsion unit!" Frank exclaimed.

"He was hanging onto it with one hand and tugging on my ankle with the other while we were struggling," Iola went on. "Then, when he finally let go of me, he went zooming away out of sight! But just before he did, he said, 'Tell the Hardys they're next!'"

Joe asked, "Did you get a good look at him, Iola?"

"Not really . . . except when I got my head above water and managed to clear my eyes for a few seconds. My face was very close to his, and I noticed he had a long, droopy mustache. I could see it under his clear plastic face mask."

Hearing this, the Hardy boys exchanged startled glances.

"Iola's right," Frank said. "There's no chance of catching the guy out in the water when we've no way to chase him. We don't even know in which direction he headed. But maybe we can spot him if he tries coming ashore somewhere out of sight of this beach. What about you, though, Iola? You've had quite a shock, and you probably swallowed a fair amount of water, too."

The lifeguard wanted to call a doctor. Iola protested that it was unnecessary, but finally agreed that it might be wise to go home and rest awhile.

"Okay, Joe," Frank decided, "you and the girls take her back to the farm. In the meantime, Biff and I will drive along the shore in his dune buggy and keep our eyes peeled for that frogman creep."

Joe agreed reluctantly, fearing he might miss a chance to vent his anger on the villainous scuba-diver. The lifeguard, meanwhile, promised to notify both the police and the Coast Guard.

In the orange dune buggy, Frank and Biff made a thorough search down the shore as well as in the opposite direction, on the other side of Bayview Beach. But they failed to sight either the frogman or any sign of scuba-diving activity.

They arrived at their starting point just in time to see Joe returning from Bayport in the yellow sports sedan with Callie and Karen.

"Any luck?" Joe inquired. When they shook their heads glumly, he scowled and socked his fist into the open palm of his left hand. "Never mind, we'll find the creep, and when we do, I'll give him something to remember us by!"

In the excitement of rescuing Iola and taking her home, the teenagers had left their baskets and tablecloth unattended. Nothing had been disturbed, but as they walked to the picnic spot to retrieve their possessions, Karen Hunt suddenly cried, "Look!"

In the sand near their baskets, someone had drawn a crude skull and crossbones!

"That frogman!" Frank exclaimed angrily. "I'll bet he came back here while Biff and I were out hunting for him!"

"If he did," Joe said, "maybe we can get a better description of him!" He strode over to a woman who was helping her little boy build a sand castle several yards away. "Excuse me, ma'am, but did you see anyone near our picnic baskets while we were away?"

"Why, no—I'm sorry, I didn't," she said. "Buddy and I were too busy making this sand castle to notice anyone, I guess. Why? Is something missing?"

"No, we just wondered who made that mark in the sand."

Frank and Joe questioned other bathers in the vicinity, but the only one able to offer any information was an elderly man with a floppy-brimmed straw hat and sunglasses, who was smoking a pipe and reading a newspaper.

"H'mm, I believe I did notice a man hanging around over there a little while ago."

"Could you tell me what he looked like, sir?" Frank asked eagerly.

"Well, let me see. He was wearing a green sport shirt and khaki pants, as I recall. A thickset, barrel-chested fellow—sort of tough-looking. I'm afraid I didn't really pay much attention."

"That's a good description, and it helps. Thank you." However, as Frank and Joe scanned the bathers and strollers in all directions, they could see no one like that on the beach. The man, whoever he was, had evidently left before the Hardys and their friends returned.

Since Biff had to be on the job at the supermarket by two o'clock to make his afternoon deliveries, the Hardys said good-bye to him and his girlfriend, then drove Callie Shaw home.

On the way to their own house on Elm Street, Joe said, "Do you think that frogman could have been the window-washer who scared Mrs. Danner?"

"I've been wondering the same thing," Frank replied thoughtfully. "The long, droopy mustache certainly fits. But assuming it *is* the same guy, how did he know we were going to the beach?"

"That's easy. When I told Mrs. Danner on the phone why we couldn't see her right away, she said something like, 'Well, if you're going to Bayview Beach, maybe we could make an appointment for later.' And if the window-washer was eavesdropping just then, he'd have found out that way."

24

"Good thinking, Joe. That would explain it, all right." As Frank pulled to a stop in their driveway and switched off the ignition, he added, "You know, we've been pretty careless about the alarm system lately."

"You've got a point there. I guess we haven't bothered turning it on for the last three or four nights, have we?"

"No, and if what happened at the beach today means anything, we'd better be on guard against trouble. I think I'll set it right now, before I forget, so it'll go on automatically at sundown."

"Good idea," Joe said.

The system used electronic eyes and other sensors to detect intruders. When anyone approached, a buzzer rang inside the house, and moments later—unless the system was purposely switched off to trap the prowler—floodlights blazed on, illuminating the grounds on all sides.

While his brother went in the house to turn on the alarm, Joe headed straight for their lab and darkroom over the garage. He was eager to see the results of his picture-taking at the beach.

Some time later, he hurried out to the front lawn, where Frank was doing some weeding at Aunt Gertrude's request. "Take a look at these!" he blurted.

"Your beach snapshots?" Frank queried, rising to his feet.

"See for yourself! These were the first five pictures on the roll."

Frank stared in amazement at the prints his brother showed him. They were photos of five men—total strangers to the Hardys. *And one of them had a large, droopy mustache!*

3 A Mysterious Letter

"I don't get it," Frank muttered, flashing a puzzled glance at Joe. "Did you take these photographs?"

"No—that's just it! I've never seen those guys before! So how did their pictures get on film in *my* camera?"

"Good night! That's pretty spooky, Joe. But there must be some explanation."

The younger Hardy boy shook his head in bewilderment. "Maybe so, but don't ask me what it is. All I know for sure is, those pictures must have been taken some time before today."

"How come?"

Joe explained that when he began snapping pictures at the beach, he noticed that the film counter on his camera showed number six. "I was surprised because I thought I was starting out with a brand-new roll of film," he said. "But then I figured I must be mistaken. After all, I hadn't used the camera in a couple of weeks, so maybe I'd snapped a few photos after loading the roll and then forgot about them. But I'm sure I never took pictures of those five men!"

"Has the camera been out of the house at all since you put in that roll of film?" Frank asked.

Joe shook his head. "Not that I know of. I loaded it to shoot some pictures when you pitched the last game of the season against Shoreham High. And then like a dope, I went off and forgot it. The camera's been lying on that table in the front hall ever since."

Frank frowned as he studied the photographs. "They're all close-ups, and the background's pretty fuzzy."

"Meaning what?"

"Well, I was just wondering if they could have been shot inside our house."

The boys looked at each other uneasily, both recalling that the alarm system had been off for the last few nights.

"Interesting question," Joe responded thoughtfully. "Here's another. Do you suppose this guy with the long mustache could be that phony window-washer who snooped on Mrs. Danner . . . and maybe also the frogman who scared Iola?"

Frank rubbed his jaw. "That's the first thing that crossed my mind. But even if he is, who are these other four guys?"

One was an old man, squinting at the camera through thick-lensed spectacles. Another, swarthy and bearded, wore a knitted seaman's cap and a turtleneck jersey. The third looked like a scholarly professor, and the fourth like a tough hoodlum.

Before Joe could offer any comment, a red jalopy came clattering down the street and braked to a stop in front of the Hardys' house. Their plump, moon-faced pal, Chet Morton, hopped out, clutching a white envelope in one hand.

"Hi, you guys!" he chortled. "What's going on?"

"Nothing much," Joe said. "What's with you, Chet?"

"Aw, still trying to peddle my white mice."

"Any luck?"

"Zilch. I went around to half-a-dozen different scientific laboratories this morning, trying to sell them my snow-white Morton purebreds. But no one was interested. They said they have all the mice they need for their experiments."

"Oh, that's tough, Chet," Frank said, smothering a smile.

"You're telling me! The little creeps are breeding

so fast, I'm running out of cages." Chet plunged his hand into his jacket pocket, pulled out a mouse by the tail, and held it up to show the Hardys. "How about a couple of nice pets? You can have 'em absolutely free 'cause you two are my closest friends."

The Hardys grinned and shook their heads.

"Thanks, but no thanks," Joe replied. "How about your rabbits?"

Chet's face fell glumly. "They're piling up on me, too."

"Never mind, old buddy—you'll get rich yet," said Frank, clapping him on the shoulder. "Meantime, what's that letter you've got there?"

"It's for your dad. Somebody asked me to bring it over."

Frank took the envelope curiously. It was addressed in red pencil with hand-printed letters that read:

FENTON HARDY (URGENT!!!)
BOB

"Who's Bob?" Joe asked, glancing over his brother's shoulder.

"Search me. Who gave you this, Chet?"

The boy shrugged. "He didn't tell me his name, and I never saw him before. He stopped by the farm last night and said no one was home at your place . . ."

"That's not so," Joe broke in. "We were home all evening, weren't we, Frank?"

"All night."

"Well, anyhow, that's what the man told me," Chet said with another shrug. "He also said it was too important to leave unguarded in your mailbox, so he gave me a buck to deliver it personally."

"Boy, this poses a problem," Frank said worriedly. "Dad's out of the country right now. He's down in South America, and we don't even know how to get in touch with him."

"But it's urgent!" Joe glanced at his brother. "Do you think we should take a peek inside, Frank?"

"We can't—at least not without breaking the flap. The envelope's sealed." Frank frowned and ran his fingers through his dark hair. "What did the guy look like who gave you this, Chet?"

"Well . . . let's see." Their stout chum hesitated, trying to summon the man's image to mind. "He was wearing a business suit, and I'd say he was about middle-sized, and he had brownish hair and a . . ."

"Wait a minute!" Joe broke in impatiently, eager to try out a sudden hunch. "Do you recognize any of these guys?"

As he spread out the five photos, Chet's eyes

widened, and he stabbed one with his forefinger. "That's him!"

He was pointing at the man with the large, drooping mustache!

"Are you sure?" Frank asked keenly.

"Of course I'm sure! I know what the guy looked like, don't I?"

"That's what I'm trying to find out."

"Well, I do, and that's him!" Chet pulled out a large bandanna handkerchief and mopped his brow irritably. "Hey, it's hot out here in the sunshine! Couldn't we go in and sit down if you want to ask me any more questions? Maybe your Aunt Gertrude might even have some lemonade she could spare," the roly-poly youth added hopefully.

"It's worth a try, I guess," Frank said with a grin.

The tall, sharp-nosed Miss Hardy was beating up eggs for one of her special recipes as the boys came trooping into the kitchen.

"I trust your feet are clean," she snapped. "This linoleum was mopped not twenty minutes ago."

"Oh, yes, ma'am—I always remember to wipe off my shoes on the mat," Chet said with a bright, angelic smile.

"It's pretty hot outside, Aunty," Frank said, "especially after all that weeding. We were wondering if you might have some lemonade in the fridge?"

To emphasize the hotness, Chet took out his bandanna and dabbed his forehead again before replacing it in his jacket pocket.

"Hmph. Well, it so happens I do have a pitcherful made up, but mind you—*eeek!*" Miss Hardy's voice rose in a sudden, horrified shriek. "Where'd that mouse come from?"

Snatching up a broom, she began whacking the floor with wild, frenzied, overhand swings. "I'll get the dratted creature!"

Chet's chubby cheeks paled as he saw a streak of white darting across the floor. One of his sample mice must have fallen from his pocket when he pulled out his bandanna.

Beads of sweat popped out on the boy's forehead, and without thinking, he yanked out the bandanna once again. His action sent three more mice showering onto the kitchen floor.

Gertrude Hardy shrieked with fury, and her broom flew up and down faster than ever. Frank, Joe, and Chet dove in every direction, trying frantically to scoop up the elusive little creatures.

For the next ten minutes, pandemonium reigned in the kitchen, but Frank had the foresight to slam the dining-room door shut to prevent any of the mice from escaping. All four were at last safely stowed back in Chet's pocket.

"Now take that jacket outside, young man," Miss Hardy commanded, in a chilling voice, "and all three of you wash your hands thoroughly."

Being too kindhearted to refuse to feed three hungry youths, she set out a plate of cookies along with the lemonade, and at last the boys were settled around the kitchen table, gulping and munching away peacefully.

While they ate, Frank and Joe showed their aunt the mysterious photographs and the letter Chet had brought. None of the five faces were known to her, but the name Bob on the envelope seemed to ring a bell.

"I'm sure I remember hearing about someone called Bob just recently," Miss Hardy fretted, "but I can't place him right this minute."

Her long nose quivered with interest as her two nephews related their adventures so far. "That fellow right there undoubtedly holds the key to the mystery!" she declared, pointing to the photograph of the man with the flowing, Buffalo Bill mustache.

"I agree, Aunty," Frank said with an emphatic nod.

The Hardy boys decided to make a speedy trip back to the Morton farm with Chet in order to show the photos to Iola. By now, the pixie-faced girl was up and about again after a brief rest to recover from her frightening experience. She studied the picture of the mustached man carefully for several minutes before shaking her head.

"No, I don't think it's the same man who pulled me under," Iola decided. "Of course, we were splashing around so much, I never did get more than a quick glimpse of him, and the scuba mask covered part of his face. But as I recall, the frogman's mustache was black, not brown."

"It might just have looked darker because it was wet," Joe argued.

"Well, maybe," Iola frowned, "but even so, I'm sure it was darker than this. And also, the frogman had a little scar on his chin. This man doesn't."

She fell silent again. Suddenly, her lower lip quivered slightly and a shadow seemed to pass across her face, giving it an anxious expression.

"What's wrong, Iola?" Frank asked.

"Well, I just remembered that threat and the way he looked at me when he said it. He wasn't fooling, Frank. He's a tough guy, and he meant business!"

4 Something Valuable!

The words sent a chill through Iola's listeners.

"I knew it all along," Chet muttered. You guys must've gotten yourselves on some criminal mastermind's hit list! This is what comes from solving so many mystery cases!"

"Maybe you should tell the police!" Iola added, her eyes filled with anxiety for the Hardys.

"Don't worry. They've already been notified," Joe assured her. "Frank and I'll be okay. Just don't let Chet's imagination run away with him!"

After seeing Joe's grin, Iola managed to respond with a partial smile.

"Come on," Frank urged his brother after checking his watch. "We'd better get going if we want to be home in time to meet Mrs. Danner."

The Hardys sped back to Elm Street in their yellow sports sedan. The doorbell rang minutes after they arrived. Joe went outside and greeted a stout, well-dressed woman with curly, dark hair.

"Mrs. Danner? Please come in. We've been expecting you."

She shook hands with the boys and settled herself on the sofa. The Hardys could see that she was under an emotional strain. When she attempted to begin her story, her voice broke and she had to choke back sobs.

"I know this is hard for you, ma'am," Frank said gently as she plucked a handkerchief from her purse and dabbed her eyes, "so just take it easy and let's get the facts first. What's your brother's name and when did you see him last?"

"His name's Jasper Hunt." Mrs. Danner explained that she was a widow and had been keeping house for her brother ever since her husband passed away two years ago. "Late in May," she went on, "Jasper flew to South America on a vacation."

"What part of South America?"

"Colombia. He loves the outdoors, and he's very adventurous, so he planned an extensive hiking trip through the Andes. Then, two days ago, he finally phoned me from the Mirador Hotel in the city of Bogotá. He told me that he would return home the next day and arrive late in the afternoon—

yesterday, that is—and that he was bringing something valuable."

The Hardy boys reacted with keen interest.

"Do you know what this valuable item was?" Joe inquired.

Orva Danner shook her head. "I've no idea. Jasper said he would show it to me when he got home. He preferred not to talk about it over the phone—for fear someone might be listening in at the hotel, I suppose. But it must have been something quite valuable because he asked me to arrange for a guard to meet him at Kennedy Airport when he landed in New York."

"And did you?" Frank asked.

"Yes, I phoned a firm in New York City called Gort Security that provides guards and alarm systems to people who need protection. They promised to have a guard at the airport to meet Jasper's plane."

"Is there any hitch in the arrangements?"

"No, but apparently that made no difference, anyway." Mrs. Danner said she had waited at home, hour after hour, expecting her brother and becoming more and more worried when he failed to arrive. "Finally, at midnight," she went on, "I called Gort Security. But their office was closed, so naturally I couldn't get any answer—and I didn't know their special night number."

"I presume you tried again this morning?" Frank asked.

"Yes, I finally got through to Mr. Ira Gort. He's the owner and manager of the firm."

"What did he say?"

"That he'd sent an armed guard to the airport just as my brother asked, but that Jasper had never shown up."

"You mean he didn't come in on the flight that he was supposed to have taken?" Joe asked with concern.

"Well, that's what is so strange—and frightening!" Mrs. Danner's plump features took on a strained, fearful expression. "The guard says Jasper *did* arrive on the flight as expected, but for some odd reason made no attempt to meet him. You see, the guard had been told to come in uniform and to wait in the arrival lounge, and that my brother would come to him. Jasper would be able to identify him by his uniform, of course. But as it turned out, no one ever came up and spoke to the guard."

Joe said, "Then how does the man know your brother arrived?"

"Well, he waited until the lounge cleared and all the passengers had gone. Then he went to the airline desk. It was South Am Airways Flight 246 that Jasper took, by the way. Anyhow, when the guard explained who he was, the desk clerk checked

39

and told him that Jasper Hunt was one of the passengers on the flight. But when they called Jasper's name over the public-address system and asked him to come to the desk, there was no response."

"What about his luggage?" asked Frank.

"They checked and found out it had already been claimed," Mrs. Danner replied. "So it seems Jasper did land safely, but left the airport without bothering to speak to the guard."

"Any idea why your brother might have behaved that way?" Joe probed with a puzzled frown.

"None at all. Jasper's a man of his word and always very dependable about keeping appointments. Honestly, I just can't imagine what happened."

There was a brief, baffled silence before Frank asked, "Why did you call *us*, Mrs. Danner?"

"Well, I've read about you boys and all the mystery cases you've solved," she explained. "Also, when my brother phoned from Bogotá, he mentioned that he had run into the famous detective, Fenton Hardy."

"You mean in Colombia?" Joe broke in excitedly.

"Yes, at least I assume so. He had never met your father before taking this vacation trip, as far as I know. So that was another reason for calling you. I was hoping you might have some clue about my brother's disappearance."

Frank shook his head regretfully. "I'm sorry, Mrs. Danner—we don't. In fact, we never even heard of your brother until you called us."

After a quizzical glance at Frank, who nodded, Joe showed their visitor the photos of the five mystery men. "Do you recognize any of them, Mrs. Danner?"

She studied the pictures one by one. The man with the long, drooping mustache seemed to engage her interest particularly, but after frowning at it for several moments, Orva Danner sighed and shrugged. "I thought at first this one might be that window-washer I spied at my apartment building this morning," she explained, "but I guess I'm mistaken."

"Why so?"

"Well, the man I saw had darker hair. And I think he had some kind of mark or scar on his jaw."

Both Hardy boys had the same thought—*Mrs. Danner's window-washer might well fit Iola's description of the frogman!*

"By the way," Frank put in, "did you make any further effort to check out that fellow you saw at your window?"

"Yes, I did, and you were absolutely right—he

41

was an impostor!" Mrs. Danner said that she had questioned the superintendent of her apartment building and learned that he had hired no window-washers to come and work that morning. In fact, he had been surprised and angry to learn that a fake window-washer had been spying on one of the tenants and had promised to alert the police.

"But that reminds me," she went on. "I decided to look around in the flowerbed under my window just in case that mustached man had dropped anything that might give the police a clue to his identity—and I found this!"

Mrs. Danner took a small, furry object out of her purse to show the boys.

"A rabbit's foot," Joe murmured.

"Yes. My brother Jasper had one like that."

Frank gave her a quizzical look. "Then you're not sure this is his?"

"No," the woman admitted, "but Jasper had one just like it, and I know he took it with him when he went to South America. Just the thought that this may have fallen out of that mustached man's pocket makes me more worried than ever that something bad may have happened to Jasper!"

The Hardy boys assured her that they would do their best to try and find her brother. "Can you give us a picture of him, or at least a good description?" Frank asked.

"This is the best photo I could find on short notice," Mrs. Danner said, handing them a color snapshot. "As you can see, he's tall and lanky and has a red beard."

As soon as their visitor had left, Frank called directory assistance in New York City, got the phone number of Gort Security, and called the firm. The owner-manager Ira Gort recognized the Hardy name at once and expressed his willingness to help in any way possible. "When did you want to see me?" he added.

"Today, if possible," Frank replied.

"Well, it's rather late in the afternoon, and I was planning on leaving the office promptly at six, but I'll stick around an extra half-hour if you can make it here by that time."

"Many thanks, sir—we'll be there!"

The Hardys whizzed along the expressway. After entering Manhattan through the Lincoln Tunnel, they left their car in a convenient parking garage and hurried on foot to the address of Gort Security. It was a few minutes after six when they walked into the private office of the head of the firm.

Mr. Ira Gort, a square-jawed man with close-cropped, silver-blond hair, shook hands with the boys and invited them to sit down. Instead, Joe whirled around and went dashing out of the office!

5 Airport Trail

Frank and Ira Gort were mystified by Joe's abrupt departure.

"What's wrong with your brother?" Gort asked with a puzzled frown.

Frank shrugged helplessly. "I've no idea. But he must have some reason for taking off like that!"

There was an awkward wait of several minutes before the younger Hardy finally returned, perspiring and slightly breathless. "Sorry about that," Joe apologized. "I saw someone out the window and wanted to nab him before he got away."

"Who was he?" Frank inquired, immediately sensing that it must be someone involved in the present mystery.

"A guy with a long, droopy mustache," Joe replied. "He was standing right across the street, looking up at this office, and I think he saw that I'd noticed him. Anyhow, when I came out of the building, he took off like a jackrabbit! I tried going after him, but the traffic was very heavy and by the time I got across the street, he was out of sight!"

Ira Gort looked baffled by all this, so Frank hastily explained the events leading up to their visit.

"Was this guy dark-haired or light-haired, Joe?" the elder Hardy boy asked, turning to his brother.

"Dark-haired," Joe said. "He could have been the window-washer or the frogman who scared Iola."

When the Hardys questioned Mr. Gort about Jasper Hunt, the security man's story bore out what Orva Danner had already told them. He was unable to add any additional facts about the case.

"You must have had a lot of experience in investigative work, Mr. Gort," Frank commented. "What's your opinion about Jasper Hunt's disappearance?"

The security man frowned thoughtfully and leaned back in his chair, toying with an odd-looking pen that he took from his pocket. "Speaking off the top of my head, I'd have to say it sounds like a case of amnesia," he replied. "In other words, a form of mental illness where the person forgets who he is and all about his past life."

"But he knew enough to claim his luggage," Joe objected, "and surely he'd be carrying some form of I.D. in his wallet that would tell him who he is."

"True, but amnesia doesn't necessarily strike all at once. The first symptom might have been forgetting there was a bodyguard waiting to meet him in the airport lounge. Then, after leaving the airport, he might have gradually realized that he couldn't remember his own name."

"But in that case, wouldn't he check his wallet for identification?"

"He might, but maybe that's all it would tell him—just his name and address. Many amnesia victims become embarrassed by their plight. They feel foolish about going up to the police and admitting they don't know who they are. So rather than try to find his own phone number and call home, Hunt might have wandered around the city while he struggled to recover his memory. And I don't need to tell you, New York City can be a dangerous place for helpless strangers to get lost in."

The Hardys thought that Gort's explanation was a bit far-fetched, but not impossible.

"Your father has probably investigated cases of disappearance," the security man went on. "Maybe you fellows have handled a few yourselves."

Frank and Joe nodded.

"Well, my agency has handled a good many such cases, too. A lot of it has been skip-tracing work, of course—that is, hunting for people who have disappeared because they can't pay their debts or are in some kind of trouble. But otherwise, except for youngsters who run away from home or get kidnapped, the reason usually boils down to amnesia. It happens all the time."

Both Frank and Joe had noticed the pen Gort kept fingering as he spoke. Its pocket clip was curved in a way that gave it a triggerlike appearance, and the machine-tooled surface seemed unusual for a writing implement.

"That's an interesting-looking pen you have there, Mr. Gort," Frank remarked.

The security man chuckled drily. "It's actually a gas pen," he explained. "It fires a spray of disabling vapor, similar to Mace."

"May I see it?" Joe asked.

Gort nodded and held it out for the Hardy boy to inspect. "I invented it myself, although it's not patented yet," he said proudly. "Believe me, it's come in handy in a number of tight spots during my protection work!"

"It looks mighty efficient, all right," said Joe.

The Hardys noticed that Gort kept hold of the device and did not offer to let them take it and examine it more closely, almost as if he were afraid they might try to copy or steal his invention.

The security man pressed a switch on his desk intercom unit and said to his secretary, "Tell Schmidt to come in, please."

Turning to the Hardy boys, he added, "Schmidt's the guard I sent out to Kennedy Airport yesterday afternoon to meet Jasper Hunt. I asked him to stick around in case you two wanted to question him."

"Thanks, we appreciate that," Frank said.

As it turned out, however, Schmidt was unable to tell the Hardys much more than they already knew.

"There's no possible doubt that Jasper Hunt actually landed on the flight you met?" Frank asked him.

"Nope. The airline people were quite definite about that. They had a teletyped report of all the passengers aboard at takeoff, and they also checked the seating chart that the stewardess turned in after the plane landed."

"Did you know what Hunt looked like?" Joe inquired.

"Sure, a tall guy with reddish whiskers. Mr. Gort gave me all that information in advance."

"But you didn't spot him yourself?"

"Well, no," the guard admitted. "But that's not surprising. The arrival lounge was crowded with people meeting the incoming passengers after they got through customs and immigration. I had my eyes peeled, naturally, but there must've been a lot of passengers I never even got a look at."

To make sure he and Joe didn't miss out on any possible clue, Frank asked the guard to relate once again everything that had happened at the airport. But neither of the Hardy boys was able to glean any fresh leads from his story.

"Better leave it to the police," Gort advised. "They'll check the hospitals and everywhere else. Hunt'll turn up sooner or later."

"Maybe so," Frank said, "but we promised his sister we'd do everything we could to find him."

"What else can you do?"

"For one thing, go out to the airport ourselves and ask around. Someone may remember seeing him."

"Good idea," Joe agreed. "His red whiskers sure make him easy to describe and notice."

Normally, the evening traffic out of New York City was bumper to bumper. But by the time the boys got their car, the rush-hour was over. The Hardys reached Kennedy International Airport overlooking Jamaica Bay about a half-hour later and made their way on foot to the air terminal.

After explaining to a uniformed attendant at the

South Am Airways ticket counter why they had come, the two young sleuths got their first break.

"One of the cabin attendants from that flight is here right now," the employee said. "She's due to fly out again this evening, but I think she'll have time to talk to you."

The stewardess proved to be an attractive Latin-American named Ms. Gomez. "Oh yes, I definitely remember Mr. Hunt," she said, when the Hardys showed her his snapshot. "It would be hard to forget him!"

"How come?" Joe asked.

"Because he was behaving so strangely. He seemed to be in a daze and hardly even noticed when someone spoke to him. Everything he said came out in a strange, flat voice, as if he were reading it off a piece of paper. He seemed almost like one of those—how do you say—*zombies* in a horror movie."

Ms. Gomez said she and the other two attendants aboard had become worried about his condition. Just before landing, she had asked him if he felt all right or would like to see a doctor. "But he said 'No' very emphatically," she concluded. "In fact, he seemed upset by my question, so I didn't try to persuade him."

"Did you see him again after the passengers debarked?" Frank asked.

"No, I didn't."

The Hardys thanked Ms. Gomez for her help and began walking around the terminal, showing Jasper Hunt's picture to the skycaps in the hope that one of them might have carried his luggage or recalled seeing him. But their efforts drew a blank until they questioned a policeman who was standing outside the terminal entrance.

"Sure, I was on duty here yesterday around that time," he responded. "What about it?"

Frank showed him the picture of Jasper Hunt. "Did you happen to see this man, by any chance?"

The policeman took one look at the photograph, then shot a quizzical glance at the Hardys. "As a matter of fact, I did. What are you two—private eyes?"

The question was asked half-jokingly, but on learning that the youths were the sons of the famous Fenton Hardy, the officer's manner changed at once. "Why didn't you say so before? That man's the greatest detective in the business!" he declared admiringly. "And what's more, he learned his profession serving with the New York City Police Department!"

"That's right, and Dad's proud of it," Joe said.

"This red-bearded guy you're looking for—what's he done?"

"Disappeared," Frank replied. "He never got

51

home yesterday evening after arriving back from South America, so his sister asked us to help find him. When you saw him, was he alone?"

"Yes, and acting mighty odd. He was walking around like a man in a daze."

"That's the same way a flight attendant described him. She says he talked in a flat voice without any expression and behaved like a zombie."

The officer nodded. "That's the right word for him. He seemed a bit loony—or like he'd just heard some bad news that left him in a state of shock. When I spoke to him, he said he wanted a cab, but I figured he needed looking after. Some of these cabbies, you know, are real rip-off artists. They'll pick up innocent visitors who've never been in New York before, drive 'em into the city, and then soak 'em for several hundred bucks for the ride! So I steered the guy to a taxi with a driver I knew was honest."

"Any chance of us locating that driver?" Joe asked hopefully.

"Sure, no problem. I don't see him around here right now, but I'll call his company." The policeman telephoned from the lobby, then reported to the boys. "The radio dispatcher says he's somewhere in Brooklyn, but he'll send him right out here."

Fifteen minutes later, the taxi pulled up at the

terminal. The helpful police officer introduced its bald-headed driver, Irv Kaplan, to the Hardy boys. He seemed delighted to meet them.

"Hey, I've heard of you fellows and your father, too!" he exclaimed. "What can I do for you?"

"They're trying to trace that red-whiskered guy you picked up here yesterday evening," said the officer.

"Can you remember the address where you took him?" Frank asked.

"Sure thing. Hop in and I'll drive you there!"

6 Closet Clue

"We have our car here," Frank told Kaplan. "Maybe we'd better tail you."

"Okay." After seeing their yellow sports sedan, the cabby added, "I'll watch you in my rearview mirror. If you want me to pull over for any reason, just wave your hand."

City-bound traffic was fairly sparse at that hour, and the ride proceeded without incident. Kaplan led the way back into Manhattan and finally stopped in front of a slummy-looking rooming house in the district known as the East Village.

The Hardys tried to tip the cabbie, but he brushed their money aside with a grin. "I'll settle for your autographs. And if I ever need any detecting done, I'll expect you guys to give me a hand."

"You can count on that," Frank promised. The boys waved good-bye as Irv Kaplan's taxi zoomed away from the curb.

The front door of the rooming house opened onto a tiny, tile-floored vestibule. Its scribbled-on walls had a number of mail slots and bells. Joe rang one marked SUPERINTENDENT.

A pot-bellied man wearing greasy work pants and a T-shirt finally came to the door. He scratched his stomach and glared at the boys questioningly, waiting for them to explain what they wanted.

"We're looking for a tall, red-bearded man who came here yesterday evening," Frank said.

"You're outa luck—I dunno anyone like that."

The super started to slam the door in their faces, but Frank stuck his foot in the way. "Hold it! If you haven't seen the person we're looking for, you'd better check up on him fast."

"How come?"

"Because if we don't find him, the police will soon be here with a search warrant."

The super scowled at them uneasily, then growled, "Why tell me your problem? Ya think I keep track of everyone who goes in and outa here?"

He tried to shut the door again, but Frank had seen his eyes flicker guiltily. The tall, strong-armed

55

youth thrust his hand out to hold the door open. "You're in charge of this building!" he snapped. "That makes you an accomplice if you help cover up any crime that's been committed here!"

The superintendent became flustered. "What crime?" he asked nervously. "Wh-What're you talking about?"

"The person we're looking for disappeared last night," Joe put in. "His sister asked us to find him. A taxi-driver brought him to this address, and this is the last place he was seen."

"Either you cooperate," Frank added grimly, "or we'll call the police. Take your choice."

The super blinked and gulped, then stepped back from the doorway. "Better come inside. If you're asking me about last night—okay—I did rent a room to somebody. He paid me ten bucks in advance just to use it overnight. But he wasn't any tall guy with a red beard like you're looking for. And he's not here now, anyway."

"How do you know?" Joe asked.

"'Cause I checked up this morning. He's gone."

Frank said, "That doesn't prove you didn't have a red-bearded visitor."

The pot-bellied man shrugged sullenly. "Maybe not. How'm I supposed to know?"

"Let's take a look and find out. It's always possible one of them may have dropped something or left some other trace."

The super hesitated and glared at the boys as if trying to think up some reason for refusing, but he finally gave in. "All right. Come on and see for yourselves."

He led the way to a back room on the ground floor and unlocked the door with his master key. Inside, the boys saw a few shabby pieces of furniture on a threadbare carpet.

Frank pointed to the rickety bed, which showed no sign of having been slept in recently. "Did you make that up this morning?"

The superintendent shook his head. "Didn't have to—he hadn't used it."

At one end of the room was an alcove containing a sink with a single faucet, two empty shelves, and a small gas range, blackened and crusted from years of use. Joe walked to the alcove to glance into the plastic wastebasket that was standing in one corner. He also opened the closet door beside the sink, then gasped and recoiled slightly.

"Uh—oh! Take a look in here, Frank!"

Frank whistled under his breath as his eyes followed Joe's pointing finger. On the floor of the closet, half-leaning against one wall, was a crumpled body! It was a red-bearded man, with his folded legs

57

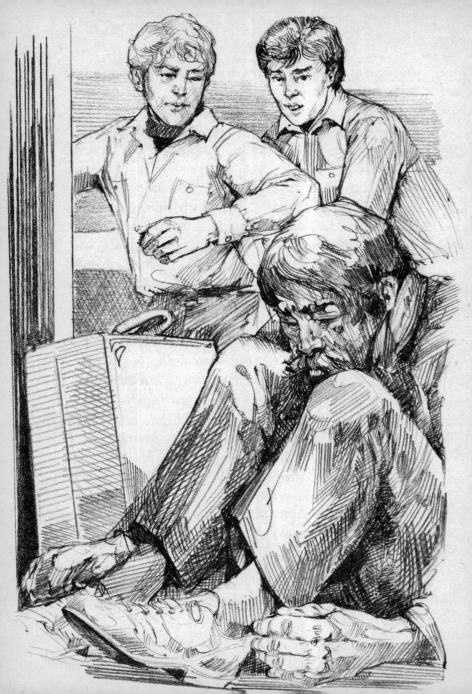

drawn up to his chest and his head sagging on his knees. A suitcase had been crammed into the small space beside him.

The super stared with horrified eyes and open mouth as Frank hastily checked the man's pulse.

"He's still alive! Help me get him out of here, Joe!"

Between them, the two boys lifted the unconscious man out of the closet and lugged him over to the bed. Frank loosened his tie and rubbed his wrists, but the man showed no sign of reviving.

Joe, meanwhile, had noticed a large lump and contusion near the back of his head. "It looks like he got knocked out."

Frank nodded, tight-lipped. "Whoever was here probably hit him from behind as he walked into the room and then dragged him over to the closet later on. This man must be in a coma from being unconscious so long."

Turning to the super, who was looking on without offering to help in any way, Frank said curtly, "Call the police and an ambulance! And make it snappy!"

A look of fear swept over the superintendent's face. "N-No—wait!" he mumbled. "Why go asking for trouble? Maybe the guy will come to by himself if we just let him lie there a while."

"Don't be stupid!" Frank retorted. "This man

may have suffered a concussion or a brain injury. He needs medical attention as soon as possible!"

"What about me?" the super whined. "I could get hurt, too! That guy who rented the room warned me to keep my mouth shut if anyone came around asking questions—otherwise I'd wind up in real bad trouble!"

"You're already in trouble," said Joe. "What did the guy look like?"

"Tough—plenty tough! Not all that tall, but real husky and heavyset."

"Well dressed?"

"No, more of a street type. Just Khaki pants and a sport shirt—green, I think."

The Hardys glanced at each other, both recalling that the description fitted the man who had probably marked the skull-and-crossbones threat in the sand.

"Never mind all that," Frank said, turning back to the superintendent abruptly. "Just get on the phone and make those calls!"

The super shuffled off, red-faced and grumbling.

While they waited, the Hardy boys checked the closet for clues. Scattered about on the floor were the victim's wallet, a key ring, a case containing sunglasses, a pen, and several other items, as if his pockets had been emptied and the contents kicked or tossed into the closet along with the suitcase. When Frank opened the suitcase with one of the keys on the ring, it appeared to have been untouched, with clothing and toilet articles still tightly but neatly packed inside.

"If Hunt was carrying anything valuable," Frank remarked thoughtfully, "his attacker must have found it when he went through Hunt's pockets, so he didn't even bother searching the suitcase."

"The thug also swiped his money," Joe said, holding open the bill compartment of the wallet to show that it was empty.

A driver's license and other I.D. proved that the victim was, indeed, Jasper Hunt.

"And take a look at this!" Joe added, plucking a card from the wallet and handing it to Frank.

"One of Dad's business cards!"

"Right. Which means the thug—or maybe I should say thugs—could have seen it when they stole Hunt's money. And they must have wanted to see if Dad was in contact with Mrs. Danner by spying on her with the phony window-washer."

"And don't forget, the card has our address on it, too," Frank pointed out, "which might also explain them harassing us and our friends at the beach— trying to scare us off the case."

His expression was grave as he slipped the card in

his pocket. Both the Hardys realized uncomfortably that Jasper Hunt's apparent connection with their father might lead to further threats and harassment in the future.

To make sure that they overlooked no possible clue, the boys searched the victim's pockets carefully, but without result. Whatever the valuable item was that Jasper Hunt mentioned over the phone to his sister, it was obviously no longer in his possession.

A police car soon arrived, followed moments later by the loud bray of an ambulance siren. Two white-coated attendants came hurrying in to examine the unconscious victim. Seeing that there was no immediate treatment they could render, they moved him out to the ambulance on a stretcher to be rushed to the nearest hospital.

Meanwhile, the officers outside questioned Frank and Joe. After telling their story, the boys were allowed to leave.

From a telephone in a drugstore on the corner, Frank called Orva Danner to report her brother's discovery and condition. Then the Hardys returned to their car, drove westward out of Manhattan through the Lincoln Tunnel, and headed home to Bayport.

An hour later, they pulled into their driveway on

Elm Street. Aunt Gertrude greeted them at the door with an excited expression on her sharp-featured face.

"What's up, Aunt Gertrude?" Joe asked.

"You know that name on the letter to your father? Well," she announced triumphantly, "I've just now remembered where I heard of Bob!"

7 *Bomb Scare*

"Where did you hear the name, Aunty?" Frank inquired eagerly.

Both he and Joe hoped her answer would provide a clue to the sender of the mysterious letter addressed to Fenton Hardy.

"As I recall," Miss Hardy said, "that name came up in a recent phone call to your father."

Joe could scarcely contain his impatience. "Who made the call?"

"I don't know. Your mother answered the phone. This was after your father took off for South America. But I do recall her saying after she hung up that it was someone wanting to get in touch with Bob."

"Come on! Let's see what Mom can tell us about it!" Joe exclaimed to his brother.

Mrs. Hardy was sewing some new window drapes. She remembered the telephone call very well, but unfortunately had no idea of whose voice she had heard at the other end of the line.

"The caller didn't identify himself," she told her sons. "That's not unusual, you know. Many of the people who consult your father or want him to investigate some undercover matter are very secretive about giving their names over the phone. So I didn't press him."

"What exactly did he say, Mom?" Frank asked.

"That he wanted to contact Bob, and he thought Fenton might be able to help him."

"Didn't he leave a number, so Dad could call him back?" Joe put in.

"No." Laura Hardy paused for a moment, her forehead puckered in thought before adding, "He seemed to assume Fenton would automatically know who he was, just from the fact that he wanted to reach Bob—at least that was the impression I got."

Frank looked at his brother. "That sounds as though he expected Dad to know Bob's address or phone number."

"It sure does," Joe agreed, then suddenly snapped his fingers. "And if that's so, maybe we'll find Bob listed in Dad's desk book! Come on, let's go check!"

The two youths hurried to their father's study. Flipping open the leather-bound book that lay beside his desk blotter, they began leafing through the pages on which their father had written the names and numbers of his clients, friends, and professional contacts.

"Here it is!" Frank exclaimed suddenly. His finger stabbed an entry listed simply as *BOB*.

"No last name?" Joe queried, looking slightly surprised. He knew from experience that his father was extremely thorough about covering all details, which was one reason for his success as a private detective.

"I guess not," Frank replied. "No address, either. But at least here's a number."

The older Hardy boy picked up the telephone and dialed the number. Since no area code was given, it was apparently in the same part of the state as Bayport.

After three rings, the call was answered. A taut, quiet voice at the other end of the line said simply, "Yes?"

"I'm trying to get in touch with someone named Bob," Frank began.

Before he could go on, the voice said, "Bob who?"

"I don't know," Frank replied and tried to explain, "You see, a letter was delivered here with the name Bob on it, and—"

"What made you call this number?" the voice interrupted in a curt, suspicious tone.

"Well, actually, I'm not even sure you're the right party. The letter was addressed to my father—"

"Who is he?"

"A private investigator named Fenton Hardy, but he's out of town just now. The letter didn't come in the mail. It was delivered by hand, and on the envelope, right under my father's name, was the name Bob in capital letters. So—"

There was a click at the other end of the line. Frank listened for a moment longer, then replaced the phone in its cradle with an irritated frown. "How do you like that? He hung up on me!"

Joe stared at his brother in frustration. "Didn't he even give you any hint as to what it was all about?"

"Nothing—not a clue. He just asked me a few questions, and that was it. All of a sudden, he stopped listening!"

Rather than give up completely, the Hardy boys went out to the room over the garage and tried calling their father by radio. Their repeated transmissions brought no response, even though they used the emergency secret code signal. Nor could they raise Sam Radley on the air waves.

"Let's hope nothing's happened to Sam!" Frank murmured worriedly. Fenton Hardy's silence was disturbing enough, without his best operative also disappearing.

"Maybe Sam's on his way home," Joe suggested.

"I'd hate to think so, if he hasn't found Dad yet!"

That night the Hardy boys were awakened by a loud thudding crash and a tinkle of breaking glass. Then a scream ripped the darkness!

Frank sat bolt upright in bed. "Sounded like Aunt Gertrude!" He exclaimed.

"She may be in danger!" Joe cried.

The two youths leaped up and dashed into the hallway without even stopping to pull on robes over their pajamas.

Acrid yellow gas was billowing from their aunt's room. Mrs. Hardy's door opened, and she looked out at the boys in alarm. Before anyone could speak, the tall bony figure of her sister-in-law appeared, coughing and groping her way through the fumes.

"What happened, Aunt Gertrude?" Frank blurted.

"I . . . I d-don't know! . . . I th-think something wa-was thrown in th-through the window!" Miss Hardy was choking and gasping so badly she could hardly speak.

"Gertrude! Come downstairs where the smoke isn't so bad!" Laura Hardy urged, throwing her arm around the older woman.

While the two made their way to the floor below, Frank and Joe got wet towels to hold over their faces as makeshift gas masks and rushed into their aunt's room to investigate.

"There it is!" Joe cried, pointing through the swirling, yellow vapor.

In the bright moonlight streaming in between the window curtains, a round, black object could be seen lying on the carpet among the litter of broken glass. Gas was oozing from it steadily.

"Good grief!" Frank exclaimed. "It looks like a bomb!"

"A smoke bomb?"

"Don't ask me! All I know is that we'd better not take any chances!"

Snatching up the object, Frank hurled it back out the window. Then the two boys hurried out in the backyard to check further. The two women followed a few moments later.

"Maybe we should call the state police bomb squad!" Joe suggested uneasily.

"We will," Frank promised, "If it's really a bomb. But it sure felt like something else when I tossed it out the window."

"Like what?"

"A soccer ball!"

To everyone's mingled relief and amazement,

including his own, Frank's hunch proved correct. The "bomb" turned out to be a mere soccer ball that had been painted black. The rubber bladder inside the leather casing had been inflated with some sort of yellowish gas that, although it smelled unpleasant, appeared to be harmless, since none of the Hardys felt any continuing ill effect from their brief exposure. The stem of the bladder had been pulled outside the soccer ball's lacing flap, allowing its gaseous contents to leak out.

"Wait! What are those marks on the other side of the ball?" Gertrude Hardy exclaimed suddenly, as her sharp eyes noticed some yellow streaks on the black casing.

Frank turned the soccer ball over, and both boys gasped. Letters in yellow paint on the casing spelled out the name IGOR.

"Who's Igor?" Joe wondered aloud.

"Maybe a friend of Bob's," Mrs. Hardy suggested. "Or if not a friend—an enemy."

It was as good a guess as anyone could offer toward solving the mystery. Only one thing seemed fairly certain—the same mysterious party who had already given Frank, Joe, and their friends some bad moments was still bent on terrorizing the Hardys. Evidently, those sinister efforts were now being aimed at the whole family!

Next morning, the doorbell rang as the boys and their mother and aunt were finishing breakfast. Frank went to the front door to answer. A tall, husky, dark-suited stranger was standing outside.

"Yes, sir?" Frank eyed him quizzically. "Can I help you?"

"I'm a federal marshal," the man replied. "I'm looking for Frank and Joe Hardy!"

8 Top-Secret Bureau

The tall, husky marshal flipped open his wallet to display his badge and official identification. "Are you one of the persons I'm looking for?" he inquired.

"Yes, sir. I'm Frank Hardy. Come in, please." Frank stepped back to admit the officer, then closed the door and said, "My brother's in the other room. I'll get him in a moment. But first would you mind telling me what this is all about?"

The marshal's look and tone of voice were neither friendly nor hostile; his manner clearly indicated that he had come to carry out some official duty.

"I have no warrant for your arrest," he informed Frank, "but the two of you are wanted for an undercover inquiry. Would you ask your brother to step in here, please?"

Frank went into the dining room and returned a moment later with Joe. The boys were followed by Mrs. Hardy and Aunt Gertrude, who were naturally concerned on hearing that a lawman had come to pick up the two youths.

"You're both wanted for questioning," the marshal told the boys, "in connection with a certain phone call one of you made last night."

The young sleuths exchanged hasty, wide-eyed glances, realizing that it must have been the call to Bob's number that had prompted this morning's visit from a federal lawman. No wonder Frank had gotten such an odd response over the phone! Maybe Bob was a known subversive who had already been taken into custody, and now the U. S. Department of Justice was putting out a dragnet for everyone who tried to make contact with him.

"As I've already stated," the marshal went on, "you fellows are not under arrest, but I've been asked to bring you in. Are you willing to come along voluntarily and answer questions?"

"Sure, we've got nothing to hide!" Joe blurted.

"They'll be coming back, won't they?" Mrs. Hardy asked anxiously. "I mean—you're not planning to hold them, are you?"

"Not so far as I know, ma'am," the marshal replied. "But to be honest, I'm just carrying out orders. I haven't been told much more about the reason for this than you people have."

Under the circumstances, it was agreed that Joe would ride with the marshal, while Frank followed in the boys' own car. In this way, the two would be able to drive home after cooperating with the federal authorities.

Neither had any definite idea of where their escort would be taking them, although they vaguely assumed it would be to one of the local offices of the federal government in Bayport. Instead, to their surprise, the marshal headed westward out of town, taking a highway that led up through steep hills into a wooded, sparsely built-up area.

He finally pulled off the road and braked to a stop near a small factory building. A sign in front said BURTON O. BRADLEY. The boys stared up at it curiously.

"What's this?" Frank asked.

"Search me," the marshal confessed. "All I know is that this is where I was ordered to take you."

Joe's eyes were still fixed on the sign. Suddenly, he gasped. "So that's it!"

"That's what?" said Frank, shooting him a questioning look.

"The Burton O. Bradley Company—B.O.B.! Don't you get it? The initials spell *Bob*!"

"Hey! I'll bet you're right, Joe! And that's why it was written in capital letters."

The marshal led them into a bare-looking, almost unfurnished lobby, where a uniformed guard was seated behind a counter. After examining an official paper that the marshal handed him, he spoke quietly into a phone.

Moments later, another guard emerged from a door on the left. "This way," he said to the Hardys, holding the door open for them.

"Good luck, boys," the marshal said, a brief smile quirking the corners of his lips.

Intrigued, Frank and Joe accompanied their new escort down a long corridor to an unmarked door. Here he pressed a button, and a green light instantly flashed over the door in response.

"Okay, go on in," the guard told them.

Inside, a hawk-faced man with thinning, dark hair rose from behind a desk to greet them. "Thanks for coming, fellows. I'm John Smith."

The Hardys each introduced themselves as they shook hands. Sizing up their host, both sensed that "John Smith" was probably a cover name to mask his real identity.

He invited the boys to sit down, then went on.

"As you may have guessed, this apparent factory setup is merely a security cover for a top-secret government agency."

"Known as BOB?" Joe inquired keenly.

Smith smiled and nodded. "Yes, that's what most of our agents—and enemies—call us. Or at least the enemies who know we exist. Actually, our original name was the Bureau of Bombs."

"How come?"

"Because the agency was initially set up to deal with internal security threats, such as terrorist bombings or attempted assassinations. But as time went on, we were asked to cope with various other problems, the result being that this is now one of the key U. S. Intelligence agencies."

"If you don't mind my asking, how does it happen you're located in such an out-of-the-way place?" Frank inquired.

"By choice," Smith replied. "Out here, it's much harder for enemy agents to spy on us without being spotted themselves. Incidentally, our setup here is much larger than you probably realize from the looks of the building on the outside."

He explained that additional space had been tunneled out of the mountainside in order to house elaborate computers, scientific laboratories, and staff quarters.

"But let's get down to business and the reason I sent for you," the agency chief continued. "It was BOB that sent your father to South America. His mission is aimed at breaking up a deadly and wide-spread enemy gang or spy ring known as HAVOC. Of course, he was not allowed to tell anyone the nature of his assignment, or who had sent him. That's why we were very much surprised and disturbed to get your call last night, Frank."

"I can explain that, sir." Frank reached into his pocket and took out the letter addressed to Fenton Hardy that he had brought along.

After listening to Frank tell how the letter had been delivered, Smith tore open the flap without hesitation and pulled out a folded sheet of paper. His face took on a look of keen interest as he scanned the strange lettering on the paper.

"This is a coded message," he announced, and added triumphantly, "It's written in a secret code used by HAVOC that our cryptanalysts have recently cracked. I'll have the letter decoded immediately by computer!"

He punched a button on his desk intercom. Within moments, a uniformed guard entered the office, took the paper that John Smith handed him with a crisp order, and strode out again.

Meanwhile, Joe had taken a small brown envelope out of his own pocket. Inside were the five mysterious photographs he had discovered when he developed and printed his film the previous afternoon.

"Please take a look at these, Mr. Smith, and tell us if they mean anything to you."

The agency chief's eyes blazed as he looked over the photos. "I'll say they mean something!" he exclaimed.

"Who are they, sir?" Joe asked.

"Not *they*—*he*. These are all photographs of the same man. He's a HAVOC agent whose code name is Igor."

9 *The Man with Five Faces*

The Hardys were startled by John Smith's revelation.

"Five pictures of the same guy?" Joe echoed in amazement. "They sure don't look like the same person!"

"Indeed they don't—because Igor is a master of disguise."

"What does he *really* look like?" Joe pressed.

"Your guess is as good as mine. His true appearance is unknown." The agency chief explained that Igor had been seen and described, even photographed, on a number of different occasions, but always in one of the five disguises shown in the snapshots.

"I've spent so much time studying his dossier," Smith went on, "and poring over what telephoto shots and Identikit sketches we have on him that I'd know the fellow at a glance. This is Igor, all right. How did you get hold of these pictures?"

Joe told him how he had discovered the photos when he developed a roll of film from his camera. "That's pretty weird to begin with," the younger Hardy boy went on. "On top of that, it looks as if he posed for these pictures willingly . . . but *why*? It just doesn't make sense!"

Before Smith could comment, his desk intercom buzzed. He paused to answer it, "Yes?"

"We have the printout of that coded message, chief," a voice reported.

"Good—that's fast work. Let's have it." Smith switched on a computer terminal, and the decoded message appeared on the screen:

> IGOR TO BOB. I AM PRE-
> PARED TO DEFECT FROM
> HAVOC AND HELP U. S.
> COUNTER - INTELLIGENCE
> COMBAT HAVOC'S ACTIVI-
> TIES IN THIS PART OF THE
> WORLD. I NEED NOT TELL
> YOU HOW MUCH VALUABLE

INFORMATION I CAN PRO-
VIDE ON HAVOC, BUT ONLY
IF YOU AGREE TO THE FOL-
LOWING TERMS: (1) PAY-
MENT OF ONE MILLION
DOLLARS IN A FORM TO BE
SPECIFIED LATER; (2) A
COMPLETE, NEW IDENTITY
WITH ALL NECESSARY PA-
PERS AND SUPPORTING AR-
RANGEMENTS; (3) ASSUR-
ANCE OF FULL PROTECTION
FROM REVENGE BY HAVOC.
IF YOU AGREE TO THESE
TERMS, REPLY VIA CLASSI-
FIED AD IN BAYPORT NEWS
ADDRESSED TO ROBERT
GORE. INSTRUCTIONS FOR
PAYMENT WILL FOLLOW.

The Hardy boys' eyes widened as they read the
message.

"Wow! That explains a lot!" Frank declared.

John Smith nodded. "You're quite right. For one
thing, it explains why the message was written in
HAVOC code."

"You mean, to ensure secrecy?" Joe asked.

"Partly, yes, but also much more than that. Igor evidently knows we've cracked the code. But it's highly complex, and we're pretty sure no one else has broken it yet. So the fact that he's using this code to communicate with us is one way of showing that his offer to defect is on the level."

"And those five photos are another guarantee that his offer's for real," Frank deduced.

"Exactly," said Smith. "They show that the real Igor is in touch with us, since no one else but he could have posed in front of your camera."

"Don't you see, Joe?" the older Hardy boy added. "We already figured someone could've sneaked into the house when the alarm was off and used your camera. It must have been Igor!"

The Hardys also reported the fake bomb with Igor's name painted on it, which had been thrown in the window last night.

John Smith frowned, flung himself back into his chair, and began drumming his fingers on his desk nervously. "That's rather alarming news, too," he muttered.

Joe shot him a worried glance. "What do you think it means, sir?"

"I'd say it indicates the HAVOC gang is already suspicious of Igor. They've probably gotten wise that he intends to defect—using you Hardys as go-between—so the fake bomb was meant as a warning that you'd better not help him in any way."

Frank and Joe looked at each other fearfully. Frank said in a voice that was slightly unsteady, "If HAVOC has already captured Dad, maybe they'll try and use him as a hostage or kill him if you make a deal with Igor to defect."

Smith did not comment.

"If you don't mind my asking, sir, what do you intend to do about Igor's offer?" Joe asked.

"Accept—naturally."

"You mean you'd pay him a million dollars?" said Joe, looking surprised.

"Yes, I'm quite sure the government will agree to his terms," Smith replied. "However, I'll have to check with Washington first, of course. But it certainly wouldn't be the first time that a large sum of money has been paid as bait to win over an enemy defector. After all, the information Igor can provide might help us cripple the HAVOC gang and prevent future crimes. It might even enable our counterintelligence forces to smash their network for good. If it did, it would be well worth a million!"

After a brief, hasty exchange, the Hardy boys decided to tell the agency chief about the Jasper Hunt mystery in case there was any connection between his disappearance and Igor's secret efforts to break away from HAVOC. The fact that Hunt had told his sister about seeing Fenton Hardy in South America seemed too important not to mention.

John Smith was clearly upset about hearing this news. "Was it definitely Colombia where Jasper Hunt met your father?" he inquired tensely.

"That's what Mrs. Danner assumes," Frank said. "Hunt was going to Colombia on vacation, and she said he phoned her from the Mirador Hotel in Bogotá."

"Why? Does the country make a lot of difference?" put in Joe.

"Very much so!" Smith rose from behind his desk and began pacing uneasily about the room. "Perhaps I shouldn't tell you this, but we've recently received a very disturbing intelligence report. One of our agents picked up a rumor that HAVOC was about to pull off a serious crime somewhere in Colombia."

"You mean Dad may have gone there to prevent the crime?"

"More than that. The crime itself may be a carefully planned attempt to ambush or capture him!"

Frank and Joe felt a fresh pang of alarm for their father's safety.

"Would Igor know anything about it?" Frank inquired anxiously.

"He certainly might."

"Then it's all the more important to bring in Igor, isn't it, sir? If Dad's in trouble, or if he's been captured, then Igor might be the only one who could clue us in on how to help him."

"My point exactly," Smith nodded.

"I feel we're in a no-win situation," Joe said. "We may need Igor to find Dad, yet, if we make a deal with Igor, we may endanger Dad's life."

"I realize that. I didn't want to put it quite so bluntly, but I'm afraid that's true," the agency chief admitted. "But I must also tell you boys that we can't let that sort of threat stop us. There's too much at stake here in terms of national security and preventing future crimes. When brave men like your father undertake secret missions for a U. S. Intelligence agency, they're fully aware of the dangers they're facing."

"We do understand, sir," Frank said in a low voice.

Joe's fists were clenched, as if to keep a tight grip on his feelings. "What about that newspaper ad?" he inquired.

"If Washington agrees to Igor's terms, I'll see that the ad appears in tomorrow morning's paper."

Both boys were grimly silent as they left the Burton O. Bradley factory building. As soon as they reached home, they parked their yellow sports car in the driveway and hurried up to the room over the garage to warm up their powerful, short-wave radio transceiver.

Once again, repeated emergency calls brought no response from their father. But Frank and Joe brightened when they switched to Sam Radley's special frequency, and Sam's familiar voice crackled over the headphones.

Frank tuned the reception to full volume, then asked, "Any word from Dad yet, Sam?"

"Negative," Radley replied. "I've been spending half my time glued to the set, hoping to hear from him, but so far no luck."

The Hardy boys took turns filling in the detective on the Jasper Hunt case, as well as the letter from Igor and its resulting developments.

Sam Radley was enthusiastic about the lead provided by Hunt and hopeful that it might help him locate their father. "I'll fly to Bogotá as soon as I can book a flight," he promised. "Once I get there, I'll check out the Mirador Hotel. Somebody on the staff may remember Jasper Hunt and know what he was doing in Colombia. That may give us a lead on your dad's whereabouts."

"We sure hope so, Sam," Joe said into the mike.

The boys wished Radley luck. Then Frank signed off the air.

"You know, that conversation with Sam has given me an idea, Joe," he remarked thoughtfully.

"Let's hear it."

"Why do you suppose Jasper Hunt was carrying Dad's business card?"

The younger Hardy boy shrugged. "Dad probably gave it to him when they were introduced."

"Sure, but why? Dad doesn't just hand those out like a salesman's calling cards."

"Maybe Hunt asked how he could get in touch with Dad after they both got back to the States."

"Exactly," Frank said. "For that matter, Jasper Hunt may have mentioned the possibility of getting in touch with us and wanted to know where to call. Or maybe Dad asked him to contact us."

Joe's eyes narrowed. "So? What're you getting at?"

"Maybe Dad asked him to give us that card when he got in touch with us—and then wrote a message on it."

"But we both saw the card. There was nothing on it."

"I don't mean in ordinary pen or pencil," Frank retorted. "That's not how Dad would send us a secret message."

Joe gasped. "You're right! He'd write it in invisible ink!"

"I admit it's a pretty long shot . . ."

"Let's check it out right now! Where's the card?"

"I think it's still in the pocket of that jacket I wore in New York yesterday."

"Let's go get it!"

The boys hurried out of their lab and into the house. As they passed through the living room, Joe happened to glance out one of the curtained windows and saw that the family station wagon had just pulled up in front. A bespectacled figure jumped out from the driver's seat and came rushing across the lawn toward the porch.

"Hey! What's wrong with Aunt Gertrude?" Joe blurted. "It looks like she's been in some kind of trouble!"

10 A Threat of Havoc

Frank held the front door open as Miss Hardy came into the house. She was quivering nervously and her face was flushed. Both conditions were quite out of the ordinary for the usually prim, cool, self-possessed lady.

"What happened, Aunty?" Frank asked anxiously as he shut the door.

"Just let me collect myself a moment and I'll tell you soon enough!" she said in a somewhat strained, breathless voice.

Frank helped her over to the sofa, while Joe hurried to fetch her a glass of cold water. Mrs. Hardy, who came downstairs to see what was wrong, hastily put on the kettle to make her sister-in-law a pot of tea.

"It happened on Brookside Road," Aunt Gertrude began. "I went to the supermarket out there to get some of the bargains they've been advertising this week. Then, as I was driving home, some wretched bully came by, doing at least sixty miles an hour, and forced me off the road!"

"Was there a collision?" Joe asked.

"No, but there certainly would have been if I hadn't steered into a ditch. And as if that weren't enough, the brute hurled a rock at me as he passed. I ducked just in time and it flew over my shoulder into the back seat—but if I hadn't, it might've knocked me unconscious!"

"Why, that dirty rat!" Joe exploded, doubling up his fists.

"That clown deserves a good punch in the teeth!" Frank fumed.

The very thought of some vicious hoodlum harming their beloved aunt enraged the Hardy boys and started the blood hammering in their temples.

"Gertrude, you poor dear!" Laura Hardy exclaimed sympathetically as she came back into the front room. "What a shocking thing to have happen! It's a wonder you were able to keep calm enough to drive home!"

"Don't worry!" Miss Hardy responded, snapping out her words. "If I could have laid hands on that nasty lout, believe me, I'd have taught him a lesson he wouldn't soon forget!"

It was obvious that the boys' peppery aunt was far more upset and angry than she was frightened.

"Did you get the guy's license number?" Joe asked hopefully.

"No, drat the luck," Miss Hardy replied. "I tried to, but his license plate was too muddy to make out at a quick glance. The car was a dirty blue sedan, but I just don't know what kind."

The tea kettle whistled at that moment, and Frank tugged his brother's arm. "Come on. Let's go out and bring in the groceries."

A suspicion was already forming in the older Hardy boy's mind. It was soon verified when Frank and Joe looked for the rock that had been hurled at Aunt Gertrude. It was lying in the back seat, with a folded piece of paper bound to it by a rubber band.

When the boys unfolded the paper, they saw a crudely lettered message:

TELL THOSE SNOOPY PUNKS TO BUTT OUT OR WE'LL WREAK HAVOC ON THE HARDY HOUSEHOLD!

"Havoc!" Joe blurted in a low voice. "Are you thinking the same thing I am, Frank?"

"You bet I am! It's another warning from the gang, just like that fake bomb last night!"

"Think we should tell Mom and Aunt Gertrude?"

Frank hesitated, but only for a moment before nodding grimly. "Why not? They're both tough enough to take the news without panicking. It sure won't be the first time we've all had to cope with criminal threats, and besides—forewarned is fore-armed!"

"You've got a point there."

A few minutes later, the boys got their father's business card from the pocket of Frank's jacket and took it out to their lab over the garage.

The special chemical needed to reveal their invisible writing was always kept ready-mixed in a bottle on the shelf. As Frank applied some to the card with a brush, brownish lines began to appear. They soon formed two words and a criss-cross design.

One of the words was the name Igor; the second was BOB. The design was a tic-tac-toe diagram.

"Igor and BOB!" Joe exclaimed. "We sure know what they mean."

Frank nodded. "Dad must have expected Igor's offer to defect. Maybe Igor got word to him somehow in South America—or maybe he made contact just before Dad took off. Anyhow, Dad probably

92

sent this to alert us, and trusted we'd be able to notify BOB through that phone number in his desk book."

"That figures, all right. But what about this tic-tac-toe diagram?"

"Boy, you've got me there." Frank scratched his head in perplexity as he turned the problem over and over in his mind.

"If only Dad could've squeezed in a few words to explain it," Joe grumbled.

"No room on a card this small. Never mind, he must have thought we could figure it out eventually if we try hard enough. Give it time."

After lunch, the Hardys called the hospital in New York City for news on Jasper Hunt's condition. Frank identified himself first to the hospital's security officer, who then transferred him to the attending physician in charge of the patient.

"Mr. Hunt's in stable condition, but unfortunately he's still in a coma," the medic stated over the phone.

"What's the outlook, Doctor?" Frank asked. "Can you make any guess as to when he's likely to regain consciousness?"

"I'm afraid not. As you may know, there are cases of patients remaining in comas for days, weeks— even years. In view of the fact that Mr. Hunt's been out this long already, going on two days now, the prognosis has to be even more guarded."

"You mean he may *never* come to?"

"Yes, I hate to say it, but there's always that possibility."

Frank whistled under his breath in dismay at the news. "I didn't realize he was that bad."

"Mind you, I'm not predicting what the outcome will be," the medic cautioned. "We needn't be pessimistic about Mr. Hunt's chances. I'm just stating the worst that could happen. Incidentally, the lab report showed faint traces of an hypnotic drug in the patient's bloodstream."

This information immediately aroused Frank's interest. "You think he was drugged and conked on the head at the same time? Or maybe drugged just after he was slugged to make sure he didn't wake up too soon?"

The doctor hesitated. "No, the amount left in his bloodstream was too small to keep him sedated very long, if at all. It seems to me more likely he was drugged some time beforehand, so that his system had time to absorb or pass off most of the drug before he was hit."

Frank thanked the physician, hung up, and relayed the news to Joe.

"Wow! That may explain the zombielike way he

acted on the plane and right after he landed," Joe conjectured.

"Probably so," Frank agreed. "Let's just hope the poor guy comes out of his coma soon!"

The Hardy boys got up early the next day. While Frank made breakfast, Joe hurried out to the newsstand on the corner to get the morning edition of the *Bayport News*.

"The ad's in!" he reported when he returned, fingering a notice in the classified section. Frank read it eagerly.

ROBERT GORE. YOU WILL BE WELCOME TO STAY AT UNCLE'S HOUSE. PLEASE LET US KNOW SOON SO WE CAN MAKE THE NECESSARY ARRANGEMENTS.

"How to make a million bucks in one easy lesson," Joe commented wryly.

The two youths continued discussing the case as they polished off the bacon and eggs that Frank had dished up. Joe was just mopping his plate with a last piece of toast when they heard a double knock at the front door.

"It must be one of the guys," Frank guessed, getting up to answer it.

Their visitor turned out to be Tony Prito, a hard-slugging outfielder on the Bayport High base-ball team. A pickup truck bearing the name of his father's construction company stood parked at the curb.

"What's up, Tony?" Frank asked as he led the way into the dining room to offer his friend a cup of coffee.

"I saw something this morning that I thought you guys should know about," Tony replied, pulling up a chair to the table.

"Let's hear it," said Joe.

Tony told the Hardy boys that he had been out fishing at dawn in his motorboat, the *Napoli*. On his way back, he had passed the Hardys' boathouse and had noticed a line of bubbles moving away from it.

"Maybe I've been seeing too many spy movies," Tony went on, "but it looked to me as though there might have been a frogman snooping inside your boathouse."

"There sure could've been!" Joe exclaimed. "Did you go after whoever it was?"

"I tried," Tony said, "but the bubbles disap-peared. I figured he probably heard my propeller when I shifted course and knew someone had spotted him. Then he dove down deeper to keep me from detecting which way he went."

"Maybe he's the same guy who scared Iola!" Frank said, shooting a glance at his brother.

"What do you mean?" Tony inquired, taking another gulp of the coffee Joe had poured him. "What happened to Iola?"

The Hardy boys filled him in on her scary encounter during their picnic at Bayview Beach.

"Man, you really attract trouble!" Tony said with a startled look.

Before either could reply, the telephone rang. Joe hurried out to the front hallway and plucked the handset off the hook before the ringing could awaken his mother or Aunt Gertrude. "Hello . . ."

A stranger's voice said, "Is this Fenton Hardy's residence?"

"It is," Joe said, "but Mr. Hardy's not here just now."

"No matter. I believe you may be able to help me. Are you one of his sons?"

"That's right. I'm Joe Hardy. Who's calling, please?"

"My name," said the stranger, "is Robert Gore."

11 *Funhouse Thrills*

"Uh, y-yes"—in his stammering excitement, Joe almost addressed the caller as Mr. Igor—"we've been expecting to hear from you!"

"Good! Then there's no need to explain. Do you know where Thrill-Ville Amusement Park is located?"

"Sure, on Highway 10, north of Bayport."

"Right. Go to the funhouse there and you'll receive instructions on how BOB is to carry out its part of the bargain."

Joe started to ask, "How will we recognize you?" But there was a loud click at the other end of the line as the caller hung up. Joe replaced the telephone in its cradle and went back to the dining room to tell his brother what had happened.

"The funhouse, eh?" Frank's brow wrinkled in a thoughtful frown. "And what are we supposed to do when we get there?"

"Good question. When I asked how we'd recognize him, he hung up—which means we just wait to be contacted, I guess."

"Inside or outside?"

"Another good question. But I sure can't picture him coming up and tapping us on the shoulder while we hang around the ticket booth."

"Neither can I," Frank concurred. "He'll probably wait till we go in and then sneak up behind us somehow so we won't have any chance to get a good look at him."

"How about going in one at a time, maybe ten or fifteen minutes apart?" Joe suggested. "That way, whichever one of us hangs back might be able to spot whether the other one's being tailed."

"It might also scare Igor off if he thinks we're trying to trap him. For that matter," Frank reasoned, "maybe this whole funhouse bit is just a ploy to mislead us."

"How so?"

"Well, say we go through the funhouse, expecting him to slip us some kind of message while we're inside. But nothing happens. Finally, we get discouraged and come out again, and *bingo!*—that's when he'll make his move, when we're completely off guard."

"I see what you mean." Joe nodded gloomily.

"How do you know the funhouse itself isn't a trap? I mean, a trap for you guys!" said Tony, who had been listening with keen interest.

Frank and Joe considered their pal's notion uneasily.

"When it comes right down to it, we *don't* know," the older boy admitted. "But we don't have much choice, either. If we want to make contact at all, it looks like we'll have to take a chance."

After a moment's silence, Frank asked, "What did this guy sound like, Joe?"

His brother shrugged. "Hard to describe. I have a hunch he was talking through some kind of filter to disguise his voice, so we wouldn't be able to recognize it if we heard him again."

Suddenly, Joe brightened and snapped his fingers. "Wait a minute! There's one thing we could do, Frank!"

"What's that?"

"Bug him!"

A slow grin appeared on Frank's face as he listened to his brother's plan. "It's worth a try.

Here's another thought, Joe. We'll probably be watched from the moment we enter the park."

"Could be. But so what?"

"We're going into this blind, so Igor can hardly object if we take steps to protect ourselves *before* we meet him at the funhouse."

"What sort of steps?"

Frank explained. Joe smiled and agreed with his brother's suggestion.

Tony Prito left the house soon afterward, and a few minutes later the Hardy boys started out for Thrill-Ville in their yellow sports car.

The two young sleuths had been thoroughly trained by their father in the use of electronic surveillance devices. Each took with him a tiny transmitter unit with an adhesive surface, which would make it easy to stick on another person's clothing without being noticed. They also brought along two radio-directional receivers, their own binoculars, and a pair of opera glasses borrowed from their Aunt Gertrude.

Thrill-Ville was a popular amusement resort in the Bayport area, and the parking lot was already half full even early in the day as the Hardys drove in and found a place for their car.

Leaving the lot separately, the boys wandered about the park, looking at the various rides and other attractions. Their routes had been decided on beforehand. Frank carried the binoculars, and Joe, the opera glasses. From time to time, each would pause and scan the scene discreetly to see if his brother was being followed by any suspicious-looking characters.

Twenty minutes later, they met at the hot dog stand.

"Any luck?" Joe asked.

Frank shook his head glumly. "How about you?"

The younger Hardy hesitated. "Not really."

"What's that supposed to mean?"

"Well . . . a couple of times I thought I spotted a guy who looked like one of Igor's five disguises."

"Which one?" Frank asked.

"The tough hoodlum. You know—the guy in the T-shirt and motorcycle cap who appears to have a broken nose. But I couldn't really be sure," Joe added. "Both times I noticed him, he was too far in the background to get a good look at him—and I have to admit, he didn't really seem to be following you."

The Hardys now headed for the funhouse. It was built in the style of a rambling, ramshackle old mansion. Several customers were lined up at the admission booth in front. Frank and Joe bought tickets and followed them inside.

The entrance led into a narrow, curving passage-way. At each twist and turn, ghastly or comical figures would pop out at them, emitting moans, squeals, eerie cries, or peals of crazy laughter.

"Wow! Look out!" Joe blurted as a trapdoor suddenly opened beneath their feet. The boys went zipping along a spiral chute like bobsledders streaking down a snowslide.

They landed in a room full of flashing, colored, psychedelic strobe lights. The floor seemed to undulate beneath their feet like ocean waves.

"Uh—oh! Watch your step!" Frank warned, tee-tering and flinging out both arms in a frantic effort to keep his balance.

A blasting gale from a wind machine soon added to the confusion. Both boys wound up scrambling on hands and knees. Next came a maze of weird, distorting mirrors in which their reflections seemed to stare back at them like humanoid monsters from another planet.

Suddenly, Joe discovered he was separated from his brother. Somewhere in the mirror maze, they must have gone groping off in diverging directions!

"Hey, Frank!" Joe yelled.

His own voice came calling back to him from all sides. *I must be in an echo chamber!* he realized.

The lighting seemed to become dimmer and the

gloom deepened steadily into darkness. Joe thrust out his hands, hoping to feel his way along one of the walls, but he jerked back his right hand with a loud *"Ugh!"* as it touched a surface that felt wet and slimy.

The next moment Joe started nervously. Someone had just touched him! "Is that you, Frank?" he quavered.

Instead of a voice answering him, something was shoved into his open left hand. It felt flat and rather sharp-edged. *An envelope,* Joe suddenly realized. This must be the message from Igor!

He fished the electronic beeper out of his pants pocket, whirled sideways, and pushed it into the direction from where the envelope had come. His hand touched another person! Joe let go of the bug after testing gently to make sure it adhered to the fabric of the person's clothing.

Unfortunately, his action seemed to have frightened the stranger, who evidently thought Joe was trying to grab him. Before the boy could sense what was happening or fling up an arm to block the blow, a fist flew out of the darkness and socked him in the face!

He reeled momentarily from the impact. "Hey! What's the big idea?" he roared angrily.

By luck, the blow had only grazed his cheekbone, but it left Joe fighting mad. He lashed out wildly in both directions, but his fists met only empty air. Whoever had struck him had already vanished!

Joe fumbled about blindly for several moments before becoming aware of a reddish glow in the distance. He groped his way toward it.

It was becoming warmer and warmer. Soon he was perspiring freely. Weird shapes floated through the air like disembodied ghosts. He flapped his arms to keep them from brushing his face. As he touched the unpleasant things, he felt a sudden prickle like a slight electrical shock.

"Ouch!" Joe exclaimed, more startled than hurt.

"Hey!—Is that you, Joe?" came a welcomed voice.

An instant later, a figure loomed out of the reddish murk and materialized into Frank Hardy.

"Man, am I glad to see you!" Joe blurted.

"Anything happen while we were separated?"

"Plenty!" Joe brandished the envelope in his brother's face. "I think I just made contact with Igor!"

"Great!" Frank responded. "Did you get a peek at him?"

"No, but he's now wired for sound. Come on, let's get out of here!"

Still other funhouse surprises lay ahead—a revolving-barrel passageway, horrifying figures popping up directly in front of them, sections of conveyor-belt flooring in which every step seemed to land them on floorboards moving in opposite directions. They were surrounded by feathery, stinging "insects" that had the two boys slapping the air and ducking their heads every other second. Blasts of air shot up from beneath them; there was more howling, shrieking, and finally, another trap-door chute that dumped them, half deafened and blinded, into the glare of sunshine.

"Whew! What a workout!" Joe gasped.

"Never mind that. Let's get those direction-finders!"

The boys hurried back to the parking lot and took the two receivers out of their car. Each had a loop antenna which could be turned to bring in the strongest signal. When the receivers were switched on, the beeps from the bug Joe had planted became clearly audible. They grew louder as the antennas were aimed toward the source of the transmission.

"It sounds like he hasn't gone very far from the funhouse," Frank said.

"He must be somewhere near the shooting gallery."

The older Hardy boy nodded. "You go that way, Joe. I'll close in from the opposite direction. We should be able to pinpoint him fairly fast if he doesn't move around too much."

106

The two youths took up positions about five hundred feet apart. Then, guided by the swiveling loop antennas, the volume of the beeps, and the intensity of the signal strength as registered on the meters, Frank and Joe began moving toward the bug.

As they came closer, they suddenly realized that their target was a white-jacketed, husky-looking young man wearing the green-and-white pillbox hat of a park attendant. He was bending over a drinking fountain a few yards away from the shooting gallery.

"There he is, Joe!" Frank hissed, signaling with one hand.

The young man straightened up as if he had heard Frank's voice. He turned and saw both Hardys. Then he dashed in among the trees fringing the paved walkway area where the fountain was located.

Frank and Joe each slung their portable direction-finders over one shoulder and ran after him. The trees were too sparse to hide the park attendant from view. Soon it became obvious that he had no chance of getting away. His escape route was blocked by a portion of the high wire fence enclosing the amusement park.

With a furious snarl, the fugitive whirled to face his pursuers and whipped out a knife!

12 Emerald Payoff

Brandishing his knife, the park attendant lunged in the direction of the younger Hardy boy.

"Watch yourself, Joe!" Frank cried.

Joe was already dancing and circling back and forth evasively, keeping well out of range of the slashing blade.

Angrily, the young man turned his attention to Frank. But before he could get close enough to be dangerous, Joe threw a stone that hit him in the back and caused him to whirl around again with a bellow of rage.

Keeping him constantly off guard, the Hardys gradually maneuvered their foe so that Joe was able to slip between him and the fence. Meanwhile,

Frank snatched up a broken branch from the ground to use as a weapon.

"Keep away from me, you guys! I'm warning you!" the young man yelled. His face was contorted into a wolfish snarl.

But the screechy pitch of his voice gave him away. The Hardys now sensed that he was far more frightened than he was hostile.

"Stop acting like an idiot!" Frank ordered. "We don't want to hurt you!"

"Then what're you chasing me for?"

"Because you're running away from us," Joe retorted. "We just want to ask you some questions, that's all."

"Oh, yeah? Well, I'm not answering any! Just keep away from me, or I'll—"

The scowling park attendant never got a chance to finish his threat. At that moment, Frank saw his chance and lashed out with the broken branch, knocking the knife from the young man's hand. His jaw dropped open and he gaped at the Hardy boys in stunned surprise. He made a half-hearted grab to retrieve his weapon, but stopped short as Frank warned, "Don't try picking that up, or I'll clout you over the head!"

"What do you two want?"

"Back away from that knife, and we'll tell you."

The young man obeyed sullenly.

"You could be arrested for carrying a concealed weapon," Frank told him, dropping the stick and picking up the switchblade.

"I'm still waiting to hear what you want," the young man blustered.

"You know what we want!" Joe snapped, displaying the envelope that had been handed to him inside the funhouse. "If you didn't, you wouldn't have run away from us in the first place. Where did you get this before you slipped it to me in the dark? Now start talking!"

"And make it snappy," Frank added, "or we'll call the cops!"

The young man's shoulders slumped. The fight had gone out of him. "A guy paid me ten bucks to hand that to one of you."

"What guy?"

"How should I know? I never saw him before."

Joe asked, "How were you supposed to recognize us?"

"He told me what you looked like. I spotted you when you first came into the funhouse. I work there part-time."

"What did *he* look like?" Frank prodded.

"Tough—plenty tough. He had on a motorcycle cap, and his nose looked sort of bent like it had been broken or something."

The Hardys' eyes met in a glance of understanding. It sounded as though Joe's hunch had been right—that he had, indeed, spotted Igor in the amusement park wearing one of his five favorite disguises.

"How do we know you're telling us the truth?" Joe grilled. "It happens that guy's wanted by the law. For all we know, you may be in cahoots with him."

"Maybe we should call the police after all," Frank said with a wink at his brother. "Let them question this creep and get the real story out of him."

"No, don't turn me in!" the park attendant whined. "I'm telling you the truth—I swear I am!"

"Then what made you so jumpy if you're all that innocent?" Joe needled. "How come you ran away when we just wanted to ask where the envelope came from?"

"I . . . well, I suspected the guy was a crook, that's why," the park attendant confessed. "And I also know who you two are—I've seen your pictures in the paper. You're the Hardy boys—the fellas who keep solving all those mysteries. And your old man's a famous detective."

"So—what about it?"

"If that guy who gave me the ten bucks was a crook like I figured, I was afraid that maybe I'd gotten mixed up in some kind of crime. So I panicked when you came after me, that's all."

After questioning the young man a bit more, the Hardys realized he could not give them any more useful information, so they decided to let him go.

"Wh-What about my knife?" he asked uncertainly.

"We'll turn it over to the police department," Frank said. "If you want it, go there and ask for it. I'm sure the cops'll be interested to hear why you carry such a weapon."

"And I'll take my bug back, too," Joe added, plucking it off the hem of the attendant's white jacket. The young man scowled sulkily as the Hardys turned and walked away from him.

When they reached the parking lot and climbed into their car, Joe pulled out the envelope again. It bore no name or address on the outside. "Do you think we should open it?"

"Better not," Frank advised. "I vote we take it straight out to BOB after lunch."

"Okay, I guess that's the safest thing to do."

The uniformed guard behind the counter recognized the Hardy boys immediately when they walked into the lobby of the Burton O. Bradley Company building, and a few minutes later they were escorted to John Smith's office.

The hawk-faced agency chief listened to their story and eagerly opened the envelope. Inside was

113

another coded letter. Once again, Smith turned it over to the bureau's cryptanalysts for computer decoding.

Both Smith and the Hardys read the translation with keen interest when it finally appeared on the video screen of his computer terminal.

IGOR TO BOB. YOUR NEWS-
PAPER AD INDICATES THAT
YOU ACCEPT MY OFFER.
THE MILLION DOLLARS
MUST BE PAID, NOT IN CUR-
RENCY, BUT IN THE FORM
OF AN EMERALD GEMSTONE
OF APPROXIMATELY THAT
SAME VALUE. I HAVE AN EX-
PERT KNOWLEDGE OF
GEMS, SO DO NOT TRY TO
CHEAT ME WITH A FAKE
EMERALD OR SHORT-
CHANGE ME WITH A STONE
OF LESSER VALUE. WHEN
THE STONE IS READY TO
BE HANDED OVER, CONTACT
ME AGAIN BY ANOTHER AD
IN THE SAME PAPER. I

MUST ADVISE YOU TO MOVE
FAST. MY OFFER TO DEFECT
MAY NOT REMAIN OPEN
LONGER THAN SEVENTY-
TWO HOURS.

"Three days to lay hands on a million-dollar
emerald!" Smith exploded angrily. "How do you
like that for sheer brassy nerve!"

"Maybe he's getting nervous," said Frank. "He
may suspect that the gang's wise to him."

"That could be," Smith acknowledged. "And he
probably figures a gemstone will be better to con-
ceal and carry around than a million dollars in small
bills. But it still may not be easy to locate on an
emerald of exactly that size."

"Come to think of it, maybe we can help," Frank
exclaimed.

"How so?"

"Dad's done a lot of work for a New York firm
called the Winfield Jewelry Company. He's recovered a number of stolen jewels for them. I'm sure
they'd be glad to cooperate and find a suitable
emerald for us if there's one on the market right
now."

"Good idea," Smith said. "Get in touch with

115

them and let me know what they say. If they can come up with the right stone, I'll arrange for immediate payment by the U. S. Government."

As soon as the Hardys got home, Frank placed a call to the Winfield firm. He asked to speak to the manager, Mr. Lurton Fox. Fox came on the line immediately on learning that his caller was Fenton Hardy's son.

"An emergency has come up," Frank told him. "I can't explain over the phone, but my brother and I have a problem we'd like to talk over with you that concerns the jewelry business. If you could spare time to see us this afternoon, we'd sure appreciate it."

"I'll make time," Mr. Fox promised. "My office is on the top floor of the store. Just come right up in the elevator."

Minutes later, the Hardy boys were on their way to New York City. It was a hot, sunny day, and the streets of Manhattan were crowded as their car came out of the tunnel and nosed along at a snail's pace through the noisy crosstown traffic.

The main store and offices of the Winfield Jewelry Company were located on Fifth Avenue in the fashionable shopping area near Rockefeller Center and Radio City Music Hall.

On the plushly carpeted ground floor stood display cases showing glittering diamond necklaces and jewelry of all kinds, lit by crystal chandeliers overhead. Guards stood by discreetly as the customers looked at the merchandise and tried it on. On several floors above were the workshops of the gem cutters, goldsmiths, and other craftspeople who turned out the firm's specialty items.

Frank and Joe were whisked straight up to the business offices and executive suite. After only a few moments wait, the manager's secretary ushered them into his private office.

Lurton Fox, a brisk-mannered, balding man with black-rimmed glasses and graying sideburns, was eager to be helpful. "I'm quite sure we can provide the kind of gemstone you need," he declared after hearing the boys' story. "In fact, you couldn't have tried us at a better time."

"Do you have an emerald of that size in stock right now?" Joe inquired.

"Yes, in fact we just acquired one from Gamma Importers—a magnificent raw emerald! We planned to feature it in a special display of our gems next week. Actually, when we finish cutting and polishing it, the stone will be worth over a million. But in this case, where a matter of national security's involved—and especially considering the services your father has rendered our company—we'll be glad to sell it to the government for that even figure. You certainly aren't likely to find one of that size on short notice."

The Hardys thanked him enthusiastically, and Frank asked how soon the emerald could be delivered.

"It's already being worked on by our cutters. We'll have the stone ready in twenty-four hours and deliver it to your address in Bayport," Fox promised.

"Great! I know the government security agency will appreciate your help as much as we do, sir," Frank said as the boys shook hands with the company manager and prepared to leave.

On a sudden impulse, the Hardys decided to visit the American Museum of Natural History while they were in New York City. Both Frank and Joe loved to wander among the fascinating exhibits. Also, Igor's odd request had sparked their particular interest in the gemstone display.

Driving back across town, they headed up the west side of Central Park and garaged their car. The main building of the museum had always seemed to the boys like an old, pink, stone castle with a modern planetarium added on the north end.

Inside, they spent the first half-hour poring over the display of gems and minerals. Joe noticed that

118

the chief source of emeralds was the South American country of Colombia.

"The same place where John Smith said HAVOC was planning to pull a serious crime," he muttered to Frank. "Do you think that means anything?"

"It sure seems like quite a coincidence!"

After leaving the gemstone display, the Hardys began a hasty round of the museum's other exhibits. As they were about to get on an elevator, they heard voices coming from an office nearby. An odd argument seemed to be going on.

"But if there are ways to make plants grow larger," one of the persons was saying," why couldn't there be a whole breed of giant rabbits?"

Joe whistled and shot an astonished glance at his brother, who looked equally startled. "You know who that sounds like?"

"I sure do," Frank said. "Something tells me it's our old buddy, Chet Morton!"

13 Rabbit Mania

"Should we wait for him?" Joe asked his brother.

"Why not? I'd like to know what Chet's up to."
Frank answered with a chuckle.

A few moments later, their chubby-cheeked
friend came striding out of the office, looking somewhat red-faced and flustered. "Hey! What're you
guys doing here?" he asked.

"Looking for an escapee from the Bayport funny
farm—I mean, *bunny* farm," Joe joked.

Chet Morton's face took on a pained expression.
"Okay, wise guy—you may not be so far wrong at
that. As a matter of fact I'm beginning to feel more
and more like a fugitive!"

"A fugitive from what?"

"A giant rabbit!"

The Hardy boys stared in amazement. "Are you serious?" Frank asked.

"You bet I am!" Chet declared, hauling out a red bandanna handkerchief to mop his perspiring forehead and casting a nervous glance over his shoulder. "I didn't want to tell anyone this for fear people might think I was nuts. But I guess I can trust you guys. If you want to know the truth, I'm being followed by a giant rabbit!"

Watching the expression that came over the Hardy boys' faces, Chet looked more put out than ever. "See here—I might've known you'd react that way! You think I'm crazy, too! But it's a fact. I've spotted this thing half-a-dozen times in the last couple of days—a big, huge, white one with long ears. That's why I came here to the museum."

"What for?" Joe asked. "To get your eyes tested, or your head?"

"Neither, funny boy. To find out if there could actually be a breed of giant rabbits. After all, if there's some kind of growth hormone that can make plants bigger—which there is, by the way—why couldn't it be used to develop king-sized rabbits?"

"What'd you find out?"

Chet shrugged glumly. "It hasn't happened—not yet, anyhow. Actually, I also wanted to find out if it was possible to do just the opposite—I mean, to develop a breed of miniature-sized bunnies, like maybe about the size of white mice."

"What's the answer on that one?" Frank asked, suppressing a grin.

Chet shook his head. "No luck there, either. The scientist I talked to said it might be possible to do it by selective breeding. You know—by picking out the smallest rabbits in each litter and breeding them together until each new generation of bunnies got smaller and smaller. But it still might take years to develop a real miniature breed."

"Why would you want to breed teeny-weeny bunnies, anyhow?" put in Joe, trying hard to keep from laughing.

"Are you kidding! I bet I could make a million selling mini-bunnies by mail order!" Chet declared.

"A million what—rabbits?"

"*Dollars*, wise guy! It could turn into a regular craze. Every kid would want one, clear across the country—a pet to carry around in a pocket!"

"Craze sounds like the right word, all right," Joe teased, not quite keeping a straight face.

"That's all *you* know," Chet retorted. "But not everyone has such a small, closed-up mind as you do. And that's not the only brilliant idea I came up with, either."

"What's the other?"

"I wanted to set up a stand in front of the museum and give away a free rabbit to every kid who comes here. It would be a great way to get them interested in zoology."

"Also a great way to get some of those rabbits off your hands," Frank commented. "At least until you can start growing miniature-sized ones that won't take up so much cage space. What did the museum people think of your idea?"

"They nixed it," Chet admitted, his cheeks sagging.

"Oh, well—never mind, pal." Seeing his downcast look, Frank thumped the roly-poly youth on the back. "That's what usually happens when farsighted geniuses come up with ideas that are way ahead of their time. Want a ride back to Bayport?"

"I sure would." On top of the headaches connected with his rabbit and white mice business, Chet explained, he was having transmission trouble with his jalopy, and therefore had to take the bus to New York. So he welcomed an invitation to ride home with the Hardys.

As the three boys left the museum and headed for the parking garage, Frank suddenly gripped Joe's arm. "Take a look across the street!" he hissed.

"At what?"

"That guy in the doorway with the yellow T-shirt and the leather cap."

Joe whistled under his breath as he saw the man Frank was referring to. "It's the guy I saw at Thrill-Ville, who paid that jerk to slip us the envelope!"

"Right—Igor. He must have tailed us all the way from Bayport!"

Chet had no idea what they were talking about. Nevertheless, he tagged along as the Hardys turned and started across the street. They were hoping not to alarm the disguised spy, but as he saw them approach, he went sprinting off and soon rounded the corner out of sight.

Joe wanted to chase after the crooked-nosed fugitive, but Frank stopped his brother. "No sense scaring him away if he doesn't want to talk to us. He might change his mind about defecting."

"I guess you're right," Joe conceded, then gasped. "Look at that, Frank!"

He pointed to the doorway where the man they suspected was Igor had been standing. Chalked on the wall on one side of the doorway was a criss-cross design like a tic-tac-toe diagram!

"The same mark Dad put on his card in invisible ink!" Frank exclaimed.

The Hardys quickly filled Chet in on the latest developments in the mysterious case of the HAVOC agent who had first contacted them through the coded letter dropped off at the Morton farmhouse.

"You think Igor chalked that tic-tac-toe sign there just now?" Chet asked, wide-eyed.

"Who else?" Joe said, then glanced at his brother. "Do you suppose he was trying to tell us something, Frank?"

"He must have been"—the older Hardy boy scratched his head in perplexity—"but don't ask me what!"

Joe took the wheel when they drove back to Bayport. He kept a sharp lookout in the rearview mirror, but neither he nor Frank could detect any sign that they were being followed.

As the Hardys' yellow sports car stopped at the Mortons' to let Chet off, Iola hurried out of the pleasant old farmhouse. Her pretty face bore an anxious expression, and she was clutching a toy in one hand.

"What's wrong, Sis?" Chet asked.

"Look what came in the mail," she replied, holding out the toy.

"A frogman doll!" Frank exclaimed, taking the scuba-costumed figure from Iola.

Joe's eyebrows shot up as he saw the letter painted on the front of the doll's wetsuit. "H— for HAVOC!"

The two brothers looked at each other uneasily,

both wondering if this was another move by the terrorist gang in their ongoing war of nerves against the Hardys.

"Does this have anything to do with that frogman who scared me at the beach?" Iola asked, watching their faces.

"It sure looks that way," Joe admitted reluctantly. "Did you notice any name on the package before you unwrapped it?"

Iola shook her head. "And there was no note or card inside."

"It was probably just sent to frighten you." Frank's face was grave as he added, "All the same, Iola, maybe it would be better if you didn't go out alone anywhere until Joe and I have cracked this case."

The unpleasant incident reminded the Hardy boys of the mysterious bubbles that Tony Prito had seen moving away from their boathouse. Instead of heading straight home to Elm Street, they veered off down to the harbor to check out the situation.

Leaving their car parked nearby, they unlocked the boathouse door and looked around inside. Their speedboat, the *Sleuth*, was neatly moored in its slip, and their various tools and equipment were all in their usual places around the walkway.

"Everything looks okay," Frank remarked cautiously.

In the momentary silence that followed, both boys' expressions changed as they suddenly became aware of a ticking sound.

"It's a bomb!" Joe cried, his face paling.

14 A Call for Help!

The Hardys searched about frantically. Guided by the faint but alarming *tick-tick-tick*, they soon zeroed-in on its source.

"Here it is!" Frank blurted, snatching up a varnish tin. His brow puckered into an anxious frown as he peered at its contents.

The can, that had been empty except for a handful of assorted nuts and bolts, now held a thick lump of a pink, puttylike substance. It was connected by wires to something resembling the inside of an alarm clock. The sinister ticking sound was coming from the clockwork mechanism.

"What's that pink stuff—plastic explosive?" Joe queried breathlessly.

"Maybe." Without pausing, Frank darted to the outboard end of the walkway, unlatched and flung up the counterweighted sliding door of the boathouse, and hurled the varnish tin far out into the water.

"Whew! That's a relief!" Joe murmured, raising a forearm to wipe the perspiration off his forehead.

Seeing his brother's expression, he added in a puzzled voice, "What did you mean by *maybe?*"

Frank shrugged and ran his fingers through his dark hair. "Maybe I'm wrong, but . . . well, somehow that bomb looked phony to me."

"How come?"

"There was definitely a voice-activating switch hooked up to the clockwork . . ."

"Sure," Joe broke in with an understanding nod, "to start the timer mechanism going as soon as anyone came in here and spoke out loud. That way, whoever planted the thing figured he could make sure we got blown up when the bomb went off!"

"Right—at least that's how it *looks*," Frank agreed. "But I didn't see a detonator—and you'd sure need a blasting cap or something of that sort to set off the plastic explosive . . . if that pink stuff really *was* plastic explosive."

Joe stared at his brother uncertainly. "I don't get

it. Why would the HAVOC gang go to this much trouble to plant a phony bomb?"

"Don't ask me. Maybe for the same reason they tossed that stone in Aunt Gertrude's window and sent Iola that frogman doll—to scare us out of helping Igor."

Joe frowned and rubbed his jaw. "Yes, that could be the answer, all right. I guess we're pretty lucky, Frank. The thing might've gone boom right under our noses!"

"You can say that again!"

Both boys looked out through the open doorway of the boathouse when they heard their names called across the water. A motorboat was putt-putting toward them.

"It's the *Napoli!*" Joe exclaimed.

Tony Prito at the wheel was shouting at them through his cupped hands. The Hardys could see Phil Cohen seated in the cockpit beside him.

"Are you guys going out?" Tony inquired.

"Nope, we only came here to check on that frogman story you told us this morning," Frank informed him.

"Find anything?"

"Sure did! We heard a ticking noise and spotted a fake bomb—at least I *think* it was a fake."

Tony and Phil were startled as they heard about the contents of the varnish can.

130

"Wow! Too bad you couldn't take it to the police bomb squad and have them check it out!" Phil exclaimed.

"Better be safe than sorry, but I guess we'll never know for sure now," Frank said wryly. "How about you two—been out fishing?"

"Man, have we ever!" Tony boasted, holding up a string of glistening, newly caught bluefish and mackerel. "We found a spot this afternoon like you wouldn't believe. The fish were positively *begging* for our hooks!"

"Well, don't keep it a secret," Joe said. "Where is this prize fishing ground?"

"Come on out, and we'll show you! How about tomorrow morning?"

"It's a deal!" the Hardys agreed enthusiastically.

A few minutes later as they were locking up the boathouse, they heard a loud buzz coming from their sports sedan.

"Radio message!" Joe said, exchanging a glance with his brother.

They hurried back to the car. A red light was blinking on the dashboard. Frank flicked a switch and picked up the hand mike. "H-1 here! Come in, please!"

"G calling." Aunt Gertrude's voice crackled from the loudspeaker. "Your friend C.M. just phoned. He's in some kind of trouble."

"Any idea what's wrong?"

"He didn't say. But he wants you over at his place right away!"

"Call him back and tell him we're on our way, Aunty!"

"Will do. Over and out."

A call for help from Chet Morton! As Frank gunned the engine and the yellow sports car went off in the direction of the Mortons' farm, the Hardys wondered tensely what had prompted his SOS.

"D'you suppose something's happened to Iola?" Joe asked tensely.

"There's no sense theorizing until we find out what this is all about," Frank responded.

They soon pulled up in front of the Mortons' farmhouse. Chet came flying out on the veranda to greet them. "Great! I was hoping you'd get here fast!" he exclaimed, his chubby face flushed with excitement.

"Is Iola okay?" Joe asked, leaping out of the car.

"Well, of course she is," their friend said indignantly. "I'm the one who needs help!"

"What's the matter?" Frank asked. "Is that giant rabbit bugging you again?"

Chet's eyes widened. "How did you know?!"

The Hardys stared at him. Joe said, "Are you serious?"

"You better believe I'm serious!" Chet explained

132

that his parents and Iola had gone off on a last-minute shopping expedition before supper, leaving him alone in the sprawling old farmhouse. "I was watching TV," he went on, "and then I just happened to glance out the back window."

"So? What did you see?" Joe demanded impatiently.

"Come on! I'll show you!"

Chet led the way around the side of the house. As they approached the back porch, he slowed to a halt, turned and put one finger to his lips, then bent over almost double before proceeding. The Hardys followed on tiptoe, wondering what was up.

A few steps farther on, he halted again. A dozen yards or so ahead stood a row of bushes and shrubbery, which screened the kitchen garden from the Mortons' backyard.

"See there!" Chet hissed under his breath.

Frank's and Joe's eyes followed his pointing finger. Both gasped in disbelief.

Two huge, white ears were sticking up above the bushes!

15 Spy Boat

"What do you know!" Joe whispered. "Chet isn't just imagining things."

"Did you think I was?" the chunky boy demanded indignantly.

"I don't know what I thought, but I sure didn't expect to see two giant rabbit's ears out in your backyard!"

As the younger Hardy boy spoke, the two huge, white ears ducked down out of sight, then bobbed up again a yard farther along the row of bushes.

"Come on!" Frank muttered. "Those may be rabbit ears but they sure look fishy to me."

He darted toward the shrubbery and the other two followed.

"Look out for Ma's corn!" Chet cried anxiously.

The mysterious white creature with the long ears had already disappeared among the tall corn stalks, but suddenly they glimpsed it hopping through a raspberry patch on the right.

"There it goes!" Joe exclaimed.

Skirting the cornfield, the Hardys and Chet plunged in between two rows of bushes laden with juicy, red berries. As they rounded the end of the row and wheeled left to continue the pursuit, a huge, white figure rose into view, blocking the way.

"*Boooooo!*"

"I was right! It's a giant rabbit!" Chet gasped, bug-eyed and open-mouthed.

"Oh no, it isn't!" Frank said, his face relaxing from the intent expression of a hunter to a broadening grin.

Joe had recognized a familiar tone in the monster's voice. "I bet it's that big funny bunny, Biff Hooper!"

Loud guffaws of laughter exploded from somewhere behind the raspberry bushes, and three more figures burst out of hiding. Like Biff, who was already doffing his rabbit head, they were Bayport High students well-known to Chet and the Hardys.

"Boy, did I ever have Chet going!" Biff chuckled gleefully.

"Well, ha, ha, ha, isn't that hilarious!" Chet grumbled, glaring stonily at the funmakers. "What a truly uproarious sense of humor!"

"You'll have to admit that's a pretty good rabbit suit he's wearing," Joe remarked with a smile. "Where'd you get it, Biff?"

"At the Bijou Costume Shop. When I saw it hanging in the window, I just couldn't resist trying it out on Bayport's leading rabbit-breeder!"

"Great! For your magnificent impersonation of a rodent," Chet promised, "I'll award you and each of your stooges a brand-new litter of baby bunnies!"

"Oh, no! Not that!" moaned Biff, pretending to panic. "Let's get out of here, gang!"

There was a brief, hilarious scuffle, which ended with Chet inviting the whole group back to the farmhouse veranda for a round of root beers.

When Biff and his companions finally left, Frank slapped Chet Morton on the back. "Nice going! Not many guys would have taken that as good-naturedly as you did, Chet."

The chubby youth winked. "Biff doesn't know it yet, but when I went to the kitchen to get the root beer, I sneaked out the side door and loaded a crate of white mice into his van!"

It was the Hardys' turn to burst out laughing.

Early the following morning, Frank and Joe returned to the boathouse to keep their fishing date with Tony Prito and Phil Cohen. The Hardys had barely emerged in their sleek motorboat, the *Sleuth*, when the *Napoli* came skimming toward them across the water.

"There's Tony and Phil!" Joe exclaimed with a wave of his arm.

The two craft headed out of the harbor. The *Sleuth* followed as the *Napoli* led the way toward Tony's and Phil's newly discovered fishing ground. Tony located the exact spot by taking cross bearings on two objects ashore—a distant church steeple and a radio-station antenna.

"Okay, this is it!" he called through his cupped hands.

It was a glorious summer day with the morning sun glinting brightly on the water. As the sun rose higher in the sky, the chill air of dawn warmed rapidly. The boys baited their hooks, cast their lines, and soon felt promising tugs in response.

Suddenly, the Hardys noticed Tony waving his arms to attract their attention.

"What's he want?" Joe murmured.

"He's pointing to his radio! Maybe he wants to tell us something," Frank suggested. "Turn ours on, Joe."

A moment later, Tony's voice crackled out of the speaker. "Take a look astern, you guys!"

The Hardys did so and saw a third boat two or three hundred yards away. It was a cabin cruiser, lying still in the water with its engine idling at a gentle purr that was scarcely audible upwind. An occasional dazzling glint of light flickered from its cabin window.

"I see binoculars!" Frank muttered. "Whoever's in that boat must be spying on us!"

"Right," Tony responded. "That's why I used the radio instead of shouting."

"They may be eavesdropping on us, too," said Joe. "Maybe we ought to—"

"Hold it!" Frank interrupted, putting a hand on his brother's arm. "Listen!"

As the Hardys both fell silent for a moment, a faint *tick-tick-tick* could be heard above the lapping of the waves.

Joe's eyes widened and he glanced at his brother. "Another bomb!"

Apparently, Tony heard Joe's exclamation over the radio. "You mean another dummy," he queried, "like the one you found in your boathouse yesterday?"

"Maybe and maybe not," Frank said tensely. "That dummy might've been planted just to keep us from checking any further—so we wouldn't bother searching the *Sleuth*!"

139

"If so," Joe added, "this one could be the real thing!"

The two boys strained their ears to detect the source of the ticking. "It sounds like it's coming from the engine compartment," said Frank.

With nervous fingers, they opened the engine hatch-cover. Almost in the same instant, a loud explosion shook the *Sleuth*!

Both boys felt the shock from the blast and grabbed the gunwales for support. But the bomb had evidently been planted so that the force of the explósion was directed downward, blowing a hole in the hull!

In moments, the engine compartment began to flood with water.

"Look!" Joe blurted angrily, pointing astern. "Our company's leaving!"

The roar of the spy craft's engines reached their ears as the cabin cruiser turned and went speeding off across the bay.

"They've seen what they came to see!" Frank hissed.

There was no chance for the *Sleuth* to give chase in its damaged condition. Nor could the *Napoli* do so without leaving the Hardys in trouble. Instead, Tony cruised closer, tossed them a line, and then proceeded to tow the *Sleuth* to the nearest marina for repairs.

Disgusted at the outcome of their morning's fishing expedition, the Hardys thanked their two buddies, telephoned a report to the local Coast Guard station, and finally headed homeward.

"Well, I imagine it hasn't spoiled your appetites!" Aunt Gertrude said after the boys had related their scary adventure.

"You said it, Aunty!" Joe replied. "That sea air really makes you ravenous. Here it's not even noon yet and I'm hungry enough to eat a horse!"

"Sorry," she snapped, turning back to the kitchen. "We don't serve that here. You'll have to be satisfied with ham sandwiches."

The boys were just finishing lunch when the phone rang. Frank's face was grave as he returned from answering it.

"Who was it?" Joe asked.

"Police Chief Collig. He said an unconscious man's just been found in a car on Newland Highway. It looked like he'd been attacked and knocked out. Just before he was taken away in an ambulance, he came to briefly and muttered our names!"

"Any idea who he is?"

"The police checked his wallet, and the name on his driver's license is Harold Sefton."

Joe frowned. "It doesn't ring any bells with me. How about you?"

"Not me, either."

"I wonder what it's all about?"

Frank shrugged. "The best way to find out is to ask him when he comes to again. Come on! Let's get over to the hospital!"

Minutes later, the Hardys' car pulled into the parking lot of the Bayport General Hospital. The police chief had already made arrangements for them to see the injured man as soon as he was well enough to talk.

Frank and Joe learned that Sefton had regained consciousness just a few minutes before they arrived at the hospital. The doctor in charge told them the patient showed signs of having been anesthetized.

"His head injury wasn't serious, and there's no indication of a concussion," the medic added, "but don't talk to him too long."

"We won't," Frank promised.

Sefton seemed relieved to see the Hardy boys. He told them he was a bonded messenger for the Winfield Jewelry Company.

"Uh—oh!" Joe blurted. "You were bringing us that emerald!"

"That's right."

"What happened?" Frank asked anxiously.

"A car overtook me on the highway," Sefton related. "It was unmarked, but the man at the

142

wheel was wearing a police officer's uniform. He waved me over to the curb."

"And you obeyed?"

"No way! The fact that his car was unmarked struck me as fishy, so I stepped on the gas and tried to get away from him. But he had too much power. He pulled right alongside me and fired some sort of strange gun at me through the open window."

"Was it a knockout-gas pellet?" Joe asked.

"It must have been. As soon as I sniffed it, I started getting woozy. I lost control of the car and spun off the road. That's when I hit my head."

Frank asked, "Do you remember anything after that?"

Sefton shrugged and shook his head, his face glum. "Not much. I have a dim recollection of the phony cop opening my car door and reaching inside. That's when he must have taken the parcel. It was lying on the seat beside me."

"You mean the parcel containing the gemstone?"

"That's right. After that, everything's blank. When I came to, the emerald was gone!"

16 *Report from Bogotá*

The jewelry messenger's bad news left the Hardy boys stunned. Seeing the expression on their faces, Sefton said in a low voice, "I'm sorry this happened, boys. But you don't have to worry. The loss will be covered by insurance."

"Sure, we understand," Frank said. "And don't let it get you down, either. It wasn't your fault."

Outside in the hall, however, the Hardys made no attempt to hide their dismay from each other, nor to play down the seriousness of the situation.

"Igor said his offer to defect might not hold for more than three days," Joe muttered, "and one of those days is already up."

Frank nodded grimly. "What's more, he may be

the only one who can help us find Dad. This could really be trouble, Joe."

"Do you think they'll be able to locate another million-dollar emerald in two days?"

"I don't know, but we'd better notify John Smith pronto!"

The Hardys drove straight to the Burton O. Bradley Company building west of town. The agency chief received them promptly in his office. As he listened to the boys' story, Smith's face took on a disapproving frown.

"This robbery wasn't just a lucky hit," he commented, drumming his fingers on his desk. "The thief must have known about the emerald shipment in advance."

"There's not much doubt about that, sir," Frank concurred. "From what the messenger told us, he didn't even bother to ask any questions—just gassed him and snatched the parcel containing the gem."

"Do you have any idea how word leaked out, or who might have tipped off the thief?"

The Hardys shook their heads unhappily.

"There was mighty poor security somewhere along the line!" Smith declared.

"What about finding another suitable emerald to meet Igor's terms?" Joe inquired.

"Don't worry about that. From here on, the bureau will handle everything." As he rose from his chair, the gaunt, worried-looking agency chief brushed back his thinning dark hair and added harshly, "Let's just hope we can find one in time!"

The Hardy boys drove home to Elm Street in glum silence. Both were depressed by the theft of the emerald and John Smith's reaction to the crime. As they pulled into the driveway, Joe saw a red light flashing from the window of the room over the garage.

"Hey, there's a radio transmission coming in, Frank!"

The young sleuths bounded up the garage stairway, two steps at a time. Frank switched on the transceiver, and the voice of their father's number-one operative came over the loudspeaker.

"SR calling Bayport. Do you read me?"

"Loud and clear, Sam. Where are you sending from?"

"Bogotá, Frank. I suggest we use the scramblers for this conversation."

The older Hardy boy flicked a switch on the console, activating the circuitry which scrambled and unscrambled the outgoing and incoming signals. "Go ahead, Sam. What's up?"

"I've just checked out the Mirador Hotel—the

146

place where you said Jasper Hunt stayed before flying home to New York."

"Right, we remember. Did you turn up anything interesting?" Frank asked.

"Mighty interesting!" the operative responded. "One of the desk clerks remembered that just as Hunt was checking out, there was an odd call from the switchboard operator. She said a Mr. Hardy wanted to talk to him."

"Whereabouts?" Joe broke in excitedly, speaking into the microphone over Frank's shoulder.

"Right there in the hotel."

"Did the desk clerk actually see Dad?"

"No. The operator said that this Mr. Hardy was waiting in a corner of the lobby near the house phones, but the way the hotel lobby's arranged, that's not within view of the registration desk."

Frank said, "So what happened?"

"Well, according to the clerk, Jasper Hunt excused himself and walked across the lobby to see his visitor. Then about ten minutes later, he came back to finish checking out and paying his bill. But he was acting rather strangely and seemed sort of dazed."

The Hardy boys exchanged startled looks.

"What do you think, Sam—was his visitor really Dad?" Frank asked over the radio.

"I doubt it very much," Radley replied. "There's

an alcove in that corner of the lobby, and it's screened by potted palms so that guests using the house phones will have privacy. The visitor probably picked that spot on purpose so he wouldn't be seen. Yet he didn't hesitate to identify himself over the phone as Mr. Hardy with no caution at all. In that case, why not walk right up to the desk? It doesn't make sense. My hunch is that some impostor was just using the name as bait. The whole incident seems fishy to me."

The Hardy boys agreed.

"You've still had no word from Dad yourself?" Joe asked.

"Negative. But I intend to stay on and keep looking."

"Good!" the brothers chorused into the microphone. After another minute of conversation, Sam Radley ended his transmission and signed off.

Despite the fact that their father's fate remained a mystery, the Hardy boys were excited and encouraged by the news they had just received. Both felt that it supplied another missing piece to the jigsaw puzzle.

Frank said, "Remember the doctor who reported from the hospital on Jasper Hunt's condition said he'd been given some kind of hypnotic drug? Well, that's when it could have happened—in the lobby of the Mirador Hotel."

"Right," Joe agreed. "He walks across the lobby past the potted plants, expecting to meet Dad, and just as he reaches the phone alcove, this creep jabs him with a needle!"

"Exactly . . . which is why the desk clerk described him as acting dazed and weird, the same as the flight attendants and that airport cop did."

The younger Hardy boy nodded, frowning thoughtfully as they headed into the house. "The only thing we don't know is why the crooks should suddenly zero in on Hunt at that particular time, just before he flew home . . . unless it's because they knew he was carrying something valuable."

Frank snapped his fingers like an exploding firecracker. "Of course! And you know what that valuable item could have been, Joe?"

"What?"

"An emerald!"

Joe's face reflected his brother's excitement. "Wow! Maybe you've hit it, Frank! That might even tie in with that intelligence report John Smith mentioned about the HAVOC gang in Colombia planning to pull a major crime. The crime could've been the theft of Jasper Hunt's emerald!"

"It might also explain something else," Frank conjectured. "Why did Igor demand to be paid off with a million-dollar emerald?"

Joe's eyes lit up as he saw what Frank was driving

at. "Because he knew an emerald that big had just turned up on the New York market!"

"Right! Now try and think back, Joe—when we talked to Mr. Fox at Winfield Jewelry, where did he say they'd gotten that emerald from?"

Joe wrinkled his forehead for a moment, then blurted, "Gamma Importers!"

"That's it!" Frank strode to the telephone in the front hall and dialed New York Information to get the number of Gamma Importers. Two minutes later, he was speaking to the head of the firm, Mr. George Gamma. After explaining that he was the son of the famed private investigator Fenton Hardy, Frank asked if Gamma would see him and Joe that afternoon.

"Of course," the importer agreed. "If this concerns a criminal case, I'll be glad to help in any way I can."

The Hardys hastily told their mother and Aunt Gertrude where they were going, then took off toward New York once again. The company was located in a drab section of the city not far from Times Square on Manhattan's West Side.

Mr. Gamma, a burly man in vest and shirtsleeves with rather pudgy jowls and a jovial manner, listened carefully to the boys' story.

"If it was that big an emerald," Mr. Gamma said,

"I know exactly the stone you're talking about. But how can I help you?"

"The manager of Winfield Jewelry, Mr. Fox, said he bought the stone from your company."

"That's right." Gamma nodded, looking interested but somewhat puzzled.

"Do you mind telling us where you got it?"

"Not at all. It was purchased in South America last month by one of our field buyers."

"Last month?" Frank echoed in surprise. A frown flickered briefly on his face. "And when was it brought to the United States?"

"Umm, let me see." The importer hesitated. "About ten days ago."

The Hardy boys looked at each other. Their theory, it seemed, wasn't checking out with the facts.

"You're sure of that, sir?" Joe persisted.

"Absolutely." Mr. Gamma opened a drawer in his desk, riffled through some papers, and finally extracted several which had been stapled together in one corner. He handed these to the Hardy boys. "See for yourself."

Frank and Joe examined them eagerly. They included a bill of sale made out and notarized in Esmeraldas, Ecuador, early the previous month, and various shipping and customs documents, which showed that the gem had been brought into this country via Kennedy International Airport more than a week ago.

Watching the Hardy boys' expressions, Mr. Gamma inquired with a troubled frown, "Is something wrong?"

Frank sighed. "No, sir. What you've told us doesn't quite fit in with the way we had things figured out, that's all."

As he and his brother stood up and shook hands with the importer, he added, "Thanks for your time, Mr. Gamma."

"Not at all. I'm pleased if I've been able to help such famous detectives as you Hardys."

As the boys drove home to Bayport, Joe remarked gloomily, "This sure knocks our theory down the drain!"

"You can say that again," Frank agreed. "If the stolen emerald reached New York that long ago, there's no possible way it could be that valuable item Jasper Hunt phoned his sister about."

Traffic was heavy, and it was nearly six o'clock when they pulled into the driveway of their house on Elm Street. They were just washing up for dinner when they heard the telephone ring. Moments later, Gertrude Hardy called up to them in her sharp, peckish voice.

"It's for you boys. Some young lady is calling from Gort Security in New York. Now don't talk too long or your food will get cold!"

Joe hastily dried his hands and took the call. The woman at the other end of the line sounded highly emotional. "This is Mr. Gort's secretary," she said. "I'm sorry to bother you, but I'm terribly worried. I do hope you can help me!"

"I'll be glad to if I can, ma'am. Is something wrong?"

"I'm afraid there may be. This concerns my boss Mr. Gort. I have to speak to him urgently, but I can't locate him anywhere! Do you or your brother have any idea where he might have gone?"

Joe felt a faint stirring of suspicion. He and Frank had exchanged only a few words with Ira Gort's secretary at the time they visited the security firm, and he could no longer remember her voice exactly, but somehow the voice at the other end of the line sounded quite different. In any case, why would Gort's secretary think of calling the Hardys to find her boss?

"I have no idea where Mr. Gort might have gone, ma'am," he replied, then added evasively, "I can ask my brother, but he's not here right at this moment. Can we call you back?"

"N-No, that's impossible," the woman stuttered

hastily, as if trying to think fast how to reply. "I'm not in the office, you see—I'm calling from a public phone. I'll check back with you later."

Joe heard a click at the other end of the line as the caller hung up abruptly. He put down the phone with a thoughtful frown.

Joe was right when he said his brother was not with him at the moment. To be precise, Frank was still in the bathroom, brushing his hair in front of the mirror. Joe strode back there to report what had happened. "I think the call was phony, Frank," he said.

"There's one way to find out." Frank glanced at his watch. "Gort Security may be closed by now, but try them and see."

Joe dialed the number, and a woman's voice answered which was definitely not that of his caller a moment ago. "Is this the switchboard operator?" he asked.

"No, this is Mr. Gort's secretary," she replied. "Everyone's left the office but me. Can I help you?"

Joe explained why he was calling. A few moments later, he hung up and turned to Frank. "I was right. That call was phony! What do you suppose it's all about, Frank?"

"Search me. But I've a hunch this could be important."

The boys stood there, discussing the mysterious call. They were still talking when the phone rang again. Joe snatched it up and answered.

A muffled voice said, "Are you interested in a man named Igor and a certain stolen emerald?"

17 A Dangerous Game

Joe caught his breath and flashed an excited look at his brother. "Who wants to know?" he said into the mouthpiece.

"My name doesn't matter. Just answer my question!" The caller's voice still sounded muffled, as if he were speaking through layers of cloth to keep his voice from being identifiable.

"I might be interested," Joe stalled. "That depends on what sort of information you can supply."

His cautious reply seemed to make the caller nervous. "Don't try to trace this call!" the voice barked irritably.

"I wasn't trying to," Joe retorted. "You just caught me by surprise, that's all. I need time to think.

Hang on a second while I speak to my brother."

"Go ahead. I'll call back tomorrow morning to see if you're still interested!" With a loud click, the receiver came down at the other end of the line.

Joe looked mystified as he hung up.

"Who was it?" Frank asked anxiously.

"I don't know. He was filtering his voice and wouldn't give his name." Joe repeated what the caller had said. The Hardys discussed the matter as they went downstairs to dinner and continued talking about it at the table. Were the two odd calls connected? None of them was able to come up with a plausible explanation.

"It looks like we'll just have to wait until tomorrow to find out more," Frank decided.

Everyone was up early the next morning, waiting impatiently for the phone to ring. When it finally sounded, Frank ran into the hall in three quick steps.

"Hello . . . ?"

"You're not the same person I spoke to yesterday," a muffled voice said suspiciously.

"No, that was my brother Joe. I'm Frank Hardy."

"Okay, I'll take your word for it. Are you interested in that information I mentioned to him or aren't you?"

"You bet we are!" Frank said emphatically.

"I'm not going to spill what I know over the phone. We'll have to meet somewhere so I can be sure no one's listening in."

"That suits us. You name the time and place."

The caller hesitated. "How soon can you get to New York?"

"We'll leave right away," Frank promised. "Give us an hour and a half."

"All right, listen carefully." The caller described a certain park bench near the lower edge of Central Park, then went on, "I'll stick a note under one of the slats in the seat of the bench. That'll tell you where to go."

"If you're so worried about someone eavesdropping on this phone line," Frank said, "how do you know he won't get there first and read the note?"

"I'll be watching, that's why!" The caller hung up with a sudden click.

Both Mrs. Hardy and Aunt Gertrude were worried when Frank related the telephone conversation.

"How do you know the person who called isn't a member of the HAVOC gang?" his mother asked anxiously.

"Laura's right. You two may be walking right into a trap!" Miss Hardy declared.

"How can we be trapped right out in the open in Central Park?" Joe said.

"Maybe not in the park, but what about later when you go wherever the note tells you to?"

"They've got a point there, Joe," his brother said. "Suppose we get some of our friends to go with us? They can pile into Biff's van and keep us in sight all the time."

"Good idea, Frank!"

"Now wait a moment, you two!" Aunt Gertrude's steel-blue eyes peered sharply at her nephews through her gold-rimmed glasses. "You know what New York City traffic is like. They may not be able to keep you in sight all the time. Or what if the note instructs you to meet this fellow inside some building? Couldn't you both have concealed radios, or something like that, so your friends can listen in to whatever's going on?"

Frank snapped his fingers. "That's smart thinking, Aunt Gertrude!"

"Of course it is," she retorted sharply. "I'm not in the habit of thinking stupidly."

"That you're not, Aunty!" said Joe, suppressing a grin.

After a hasty discussion, he telephoned Biff Hooper and Chet Morton and asked them in turn to contact Tony Prito and Phil Cohen. Meanwhile, Frank was assembling lapel mikes and transmitter bugs, which he and Joe could carry in the pockets of their jackets along with highly miniaturized receivers, both tuned to the frequency of the CB radio in Biff's van.

In little more than twenty minutes, the Bayporters were on their way to New York City—Frank and Joe in the lead in their yellow sports car, their friends following in Biff's van, gaudily painted in psychedelic rainbow hues.

After parking in an open-air lot nearby, the Hardys hurried toward Central Park and quickly found the bench referred to by their mysterious caller. Luckily, no one was using it at the moment. The boys sat down and casually began running their fingers underneath the seat planks.

"Here it is," Frank announced softly.

The small piece of paper had been stuck in place with chewing gum. The note simply said:

PHONE BOOTH SE CORNER OF FIFTY-THIRD & FIFTH

"What happens when we get there?" Joe wondered aloud.

"We'll soon find out!"

The bench was situated in clear view of the busy street that ran along the south edge of the park. From where they sat, the Hardys could glimpse Biff's van, which had pulled into a convenient parking spot not far away.

"Do you suppose we're being watched right now?" Joe murmured as they rose from the bench.

"I'd be willing to bet on it," Frank responded. "Don't try to signal the van, if that's what you were thinking of doing. They can hear us fine—right, guys?"

"We read you, pal!" Tony Prito's muffled voice came from both their pocket receivers.

"We're on our way to Fifth Avenue and Fifty-third, southeast corner." Frank's quietly spoken words were picked up readily by his lapel mike. "Over and out for now."

"Right."

Stepping out briskly, the Hardys soon covered the half-dozen blocks to their destination. There were two transparent phone booths across the street from gray-stoned Saint Thomas' Church and within view of the modernistic facade of the Museum of Modern Art.

"Okay, we're here," Joe murmured as they stepped out of the way of the hurrying throng of pedestrians. "Now what?"

Frank shrugged, his eyes watchful. "Wait, I guess."

Moments later, one of the two phones rang. Frank snatched it up and said, "Hardys here."

"Reach underneath the phone," said the same muffled voice he had heard in Bayport.

Frank did so and found some folded paper taped there. It turned out to be a map of midtown Manhattan, evidently cut from some larger map. Nine points were lettered on the map, forming a rough square:

A B C
D E F
G H I

"This phone you're using now is at Point A," said the voice. "Do you see it there on the map?"

"I see it," Frank said.

"Okay, go to Point E," said the voice and hung up.

"What do you suppose the guy's up to?" asked Joe as he and his brother started down Fifth Avenue. Their new destination lay several blocks away to the southeast.

"He's playing it cagey," Frank opined, "making sure we don't double-cross him and have any cops lying in wait when we finally meet."

"In that case, we must be under observation all the time—which means he can't be working alone."

"That figures," the older Hardy boy agreed grim-

ly. Both realized this made it all the more possible that the plan might end in a trap, as their mother and aunt had feared. But they decided to continue, relying on their friends for backup support.

At Point E, they found another sidewalk phone and received another call. This time they were told to proceed to Point I, again to the southeast.

"Still with us, guys?" Joe inquired over the radio as the Hardys continued their trek.

"About two blocks behind you," Tony responded. "Everything cool?"

"So far, but keep your fingers crossed!"

From the phone booth at Point I, the Hardys were told to go to Point G, directly west on the same street where it crossed Fifth Avenue. Another phone call directed them to Point C, a considerable distance to the northeast and once again on Fifty-third Street. The next call told them to go west on Fifty-third to Point B.

"What kind of a run-around is this nut giving us?" Joe complained as they plodded along wearily. "Not only are my feet sore—I stubbed my toe back there."

The word *toe* echoed in Frank's mind. It seemed to tie in with an idea that was already flickering through his brain. Suddenly, he pulled out the map, which he had found taped under the first

164

phone stand, and glanced at the nine points lettered on it.

"Want a prediction, Joe? I'll bet the next phone call tells us to go to Point F—and that's where we'll meet the guy!"

"Are you serious?" Joe stared at his brother.

"You bet I'm serious!"

"Okay, then how do you figure it?"

"Don't you see?" Frank replied tensely. "He's playing tic-tac-toe!"

Joe stopped short in surprise, remembering the tic-tac-toe diagram marked in invisible ink on the back of their father's business card, and the one Igor had chalked in the doorway. But Frank nudged his brother back into motion. "Keep walking! Somebody may be watching us."

"Run that past me again, Frank."

"There are nine letters marked on this map, right? Think of each letter as one square of a tic-tac-toe diagram. That first call was like an X-mark in one corner of the diagram," Frank explained. "Then the next call corresponded to a circle in the center of the diagram, and so on. Remember, the game's over whenever one player can line up three Xs or three circles in a row. Well, if the next call says to go to Point F, that'll make three Xs in a row. Get it?"

"Yes, I think so," Joe said slowly. "But why? What's the reason for going through such a routine?"

"It may be S.O.P., that's why—standard operating procedure for the HAVOC gang. Perhaps this is the way they arrange a safe meeting between two parties who don't trust each other, or if they want to make sure neither one has been bugged or tailed. Maybe this is why both Dad and Igor drew those criss-crosses—to let us know this is the procedure Igor would use whenever he was ready to defect."

"Wow! That makes sense, all right!" Joe exclaimed. "But playing tic-tac-toe takes two people. How come that guy who phoned us is calling all the moves?"

"You're right about the game taking two people," said Frank. "That way—say if two gang members wanted to meet safely—one would pick the first phone booth, the other would pick the next phone booth, and so on. Neither would know in advance how the game would come out, or which would be the winning location. No one could set a trap for them simply because neither would know in advance where they'd actually meet."

"Okay," Joe nodded. "But how about this routine we're going through right now with our unknown informant picking *all* the phone booths?"

"For one thing," Frank said, "it'll give the gang plenty of time to make sure we don't have any cops tagging along. Also, they're waiting to see if we get wise to the tic-tac-toe bit and whether we'll say anything about it."

"What difference would that make?"

"If we do, they'll know that Igor must have tipped us off—and that he's planning to defect!"

"Boy, oh boy! I think that's it, Frank! That must be the answer!" Joe exclaimed. Then his voice abruptly became more serious as he added, "But look—do we *want* to meet these HAVOC gangsters face to face, if that's who set up this game we're playing right now? They could be a pretty nasty bunch to tangle with!"

"How else can we crack this case? Especially when Dad's life may depend on it!"

"You're right, Frank. We'll just have to play it cool and keep our wits about us. After all, we've got the guys to help us out in an emergency."

Frank nodded tensely and said, "Do you read us, Tony?"

"Loud and clear," came the reply. "But I'm not sure I understand all that tic-tac-toe stuff you were just talking about."

"Never mind that," Frank glanced hastily at the map and read out the location of Point F. "You

167

guys drive there right now and wait for us. We're going to play a hunch!"

"Okay."

A few more paces brought the Hardys to the phone booth at Point B. A minute or two later, the telephone rang. Frank picked it up.

"Where to now?" he asked, holding the receiver far enough away from his ear so Joe could also hear the answer.

The brothers grinned triumphantly as the muffled voice said, "Point F."

"Understood."

Frank hung up, and the Hardys started off briskly, side by side.

"It looks like this is it," Joe murmured, speaking both to his brother and their friends listening over the radio.

Their destination lay southeast on Lexington Avenue. When they reached it, the Hardys stood by the sidewalk phone, waiting expectantly for it to ring.

Instead, a large, maroon sedan suddenly pulled up at the curb. A uniformed chauffeur was sitting at the wheel with an old lady as his back-seat passenger. She beckoned to the two boys.

"If you want that information," she said in a quavering, elderly voice, "please get in."

Joe shot a quick glance at his brother, who

shrugged. Then both climbed into the back seat as the old lady moved over to make room for them.

The chauffeur put the car into gear, and the big, luxurious sedan glided smoothly into the busy traffic.

"You lads do trust me, I hope?" the old lady quavered gently.

"I guess we'll have to, ma'am," Frank said tersely.

The old lady's quavering voice suddenly changed to a harsh, masculine rasp. "Yeah? Well, that's where you Hardys made your big mistake!"

The brothers gasped as they realized that the figure beside them was a man in disguise! He had just pulled a penlike object from the purse in his lap and was pointing it their way.

"This thing fires nerve gas, understand? And its effects are very unpleasant, believe me! You two do as you're told or you'll both get a noseful!"

18 Rescue Van

Trapped! In spite of all their precautions, they had blundered right into HAVOC's clutches—all because of trusting someone who appeared to be a harmless old lady!

But in spite of their predicament, the Hardy boys were more angry than scared. Their captor could tell from the blazing look in their eyes that the two spunky youths were full of fight.

"Just sit tight and don't try anything!" he snarled. "One dose of this nerve gas, and you'll feel like you've got fire ants crawling all over you! Think I'm kidding? We have gas masks for ourselves and will be happy to show you. But better take my word for it, punks, or you'll find out the hard way!"

"You're not scaring us," Joe retorted scornfully. "You guys are the ones who'd better start worrying!"

"Don't make me laugh!"

"You won't," Frank snapped, "when you find out the spot you're in!"

"What spot?"

"A bunch of our buddies are following this car," Joe informed him. "They're in a rainbow-colored van that's equipped with CB radio. If you don't let us out safely, they'll have the cops on your neck so fast you won't know what hit you!"

The man sneered. "Don't try to con me, kid. There's no way your friends could have known where we'd pick you up."

But the chauffeur, whose eyes were glued to the rearview mirror, exclaimed, "Don't be too sure! There's a van like that coming up fast right behind us!"

His partner was clearly startled by this unexpected news. Without thinking, he jerked his head around to glance out the window.

Frank, who was sitting next to him, seized his chance. He grabbed the crook's wrist to prevent him from firing the gas pen, and then began trying to wrest the weapon away from him. His opponent fought back with his other hand, punching and gouging the strong teenager.

171

Joe, who was sitting on the other side of Frank, had to squirm past his brother to get into the action. He soon managed to grab the crook's other wrist.

"Help me, stupid!" the disguised man exclaimed to the chauffeur. "These punks are trying to take over!"

The chauffeur turned his head long enough to shoot an anxious glance over his shoulder. He swung his arm over the seat back, trying to hit Joe with a backhand punch. But he dared not take his eyes off the hectic, fast-moving traffic all around them.

"Do something!" his partner cried frantically.

"Like what? Do you want us to crash into one of these taxis or something? Then we'd really have the cops on our necks fast!"

Meanwhile, the Hardy boys were elbowing and twisting the wrists of the crook in the back seat.

Moments later, the car slowed to a halt for a traffic light. At that instant, Frank got the gas pen away from their opponent.

"Scram, Joe!" he blurted.

Joe yanked open the car door and leaped out. Frank lunged after him, but the man grabbed him by the ankle. Frank freed himself with a swift karate kick and plunged after his brother.

There was another lane of cars between the

172

Hardys and the curb. The boys darted between the two nearest vehicles while the light was still red and leaped into the throng of pedestrians on the sidewalk, with hastily muttered apologies to those they bumped into.

Meanwhile, the disheveled "old lady" glared at the Hardys in helpless fury from the maroon sedan.

"There's Biff!" Joe exclaimed, waving his arm.

The light turned green, and traffic began to move again. The van cut over to the curb to pick up the Hardy boys, despite angry shouts and honks from other drivers.

At the same time, the enemy sedan had to move on across the intersection, impelled by the sheer pressure of traffic and even more violent honking from cars behind it.

"Make a right!" Frank told Biff. "Let's put some distance between us and those creeps!"

Biff did so. Then he began turning right or left at every other corner until the Bayporters felt sure that the crooks in the maroon sedan had little chance of sighting them again.

Tony and the others had been listening in by radio to what happened after the Hardys were taken captive.

"Man, it's lucky you guys didn't get a squirt of that nerve gas!" Chet said.

"Which reminds me," Joe said to his brother, "do you have the pen?"

"Right here," Frank said, and pulled it out of his pocket.

"Let's have a closer look at that." Joe took it and studied it intently. "Does this remind you of anything, Frank?"

"It sure does. It's just like the pen Ira Gort showed us."

Joe nodded. "And yesterday we got that phony call asking if we knew where to find Gort. I'm beginning to wonder if Gort may not be mixed up with HAVOC!"

"You and I both!" Frank took back the gas weapon from his brother and scowled at it while turning it over in his hand. "In fact, I'm beginning to get an even wilder idea. Gort's first name is Ira—initial I. Put 'em together and what have you got—*I. Gort.* Does that remind you of anything?"

Joe's eyes suddenly widened and he snapped his fingers. "Wow! I'll say it does! . . . *Igor!* If he's the agent who's trying to defect, that would explain plenty. Like why HAVOC wants to find him! Maybe even what happened to Jasper Hunt!"

"Right. And a firm like Gort Security would sure be an asset to any criminal gang. Think of all the industrial plants and offices a security expert like Gort must get called in to guard. That would give

174

him a chance to plant bugs so he could eavesdrop on their business secrets. He could even get the lowdown on their alarm systems if he wanted to plan a burglary."

"Maybe we ought to pay Gort a visit, Frank."

"Just what I was thinking!"

Biff dropped the Hardys off at the building in which Gort Security was located. When they entered the firm's offices, his secretary seemed nervous and agitated. "Mr. Gort isn't here right now," she told them

"Is anything wrong, miss?" Frank asked sympathetically, noticing her pale face and the way she was kneading a handkerchief in one hand.

To the boys' surprise, the young woman choked back a sob and almost burst into tears. "Oh, I'm so worried I don't know what to do!" she confessed.

"Tell us about it. Maybe we can help."

The secretary, who knew the reputation of the Hardy boys and their famous father, related that several tough-looking strangers had started a campaign of harassment. At times they would keep a close watch on the firm's offices, and at other times they had actually come in and inquired where Gort had gone. Then they had uttered threatening remarks.

"Where *is* your boss?" Joe asked bluntly.

At first, the woman seemed reluctant to answer,

as if she were not sure she could trust them. But she finally yielded when Frank said, "Look, if he's in fear of his life, we can arrange an absolutely safe place for him to go, where he'll be protected by federal authorities."

"Oh, if you could, that would be wonderful!" she said tearfully. "It would take such a weight off my mind!"

"Then tell us how to get in touch with him."

"All right." She led the Hardys into another room, which was equipped with an elaborate bank of radio communications gear and closed-circuit television equipment. After switching on a transceiver, she sent out a code call. Presently, Gort's voice responded. The secretary explained that the Hardy boys wished to speak to him.

"What about?" Gort asked suspiciously.

Frank took over the microphone from the secretary while Joe escorted her out of the room again. "About someone named Igor," Frank said.

There was a short, tense silence before Gort said, "Am I supposed to know what that means?"

"If you don't, what are you hiding out for?"

"Who says I'm hiding out?"

"Look!" Frank retorted curtly. "There's no time to play games. Your secretary's already told us about those tough goons who are looking for you. They're probably thugs working for HAVOC. Joe and I almost got kidnapped ourselves. If you still want to defect, we can take you straight to BOB. If you don't . . . well, suit yourself and take your own chances. But make up your mind!"

Gort still hesitated. There was almost a whine in his voice when it finally came over the loudspeaker again. "How do I know I can trust you?"

"You were the one who first contacted *us*, not the other way around," Frank reminded him. "Why did you trust our father to start with? You're in big trouble, Gort, and you know it. We're offering you the quickest way out. We'll take you to a U. S. Government agency that's ready to provide full protection. Take it or leave it."

"Very well. What exactly are you proposing?"

"Are you in New York City?"

"Yes."

"Then name a place where we can pick you up. And the sooner the better."

After thinking a few moments, Gort suggested a block on West Forty-seventh Street in the heart of the diamond district. The Hardys agreed.

Frank and Joe left the offices of the security firm and rode with their pals in Biff's van to the parking lot where they had left their yellow sports car. Then they drove to West Forty-seventh Street by a roundabout route, checking their watches to synchronize with the pick-up time Gort had requested.

As they cruised along West Forty-seventh, the sidewalks were crowded with pedestrians, many of them in the gem trade. Some wore the black hats, long hair, and full beards of the Orthodox Jewish sect to which many of the world's most expert diamond-cutters and craftspeople belonged. In the heavy crosstown traffic, the speed of the Hardys' car was reduced to a crawl.

"There he is!" Joe exclaimed suddenly.

Ira Gort came darting out of a doorway, visibly nervous and perspiring. As Joe held open the car door, he leaped aboard and squirmed into the back seat. Ten minutes later, they were entering the Lincoln Tunnel, leading westward out of Manhattan under the Hudson River.

For a time, Gort would speak only in monosyllables. But once they reached an open expanse of interstate expressway, with the Manhattan skyline fading in the distance, he seemed to relax.

The Hardys, too, felt safer until Frank noticed a dark-reddish car speeding closer in the lefthand lane. It gradually settled into place behind them.

"Don't look now, Joe," Frank muttered, "but I think we've got company."

Their tail car was a maroon sedan with a uniformed chauffeur at the wheel!

19 The Secret Key

"Who is it?" Ira Gort croaked from the back seat. His voice was taut and husky with fear.

"I think it's the same car that Joe and I were kidnapped in just before we went to your office."

"Then you've got to do something before they take us!" Gort said, shrinking into a corner of the seat as if trying to make himself invisible. "They may be armed!"

Frank was thinking the same thing. Although he could not make out all the passengers in the maroon sedan, the man seated beside the chauffeur was a hard-faced, thuglike individual.

"Relax," Joe told Gort. "We've got friends who can help us." Holding his jacket collar up to his face so his lips would be close to the lapel mike, Joe said,

"Hardys calling van! . . . Do you read me, Tony?"

"The reception's not too good, but I can understand you," Tony replied. "How about you guys? Am I getting through?"

"Affirmative. We've got that maroon sedan on our tail again. They must have spotted us at Gort Security, but they've kept out of sight until now. Can you run interference for us?"

"You've got it, pal! Over and out."

So far, the maroon car had remained at a steady distance behind them, as if to give the Hardys and their passenger time to realize they were being followed and thus intimidate them. Meanwhile, a steady stream of traffic was flowing in the left lane.

But now the enemy showed signs of stepping up the war of nerves. As traffic thinned, the maroon sedan increased speed and veered out as if trying to pull abreast of the Hardys. To thwart this move, Frank veered left also and stepped on the gas. When the enemy sedan swung right again, he too shifted course in order to keep it from passing.

"What do you suppose they're up to?" Joe asked.

"I don't know." Frank cranked up the driver's side window. "Maybe they'd like to toss a grenade at us, the same way one of them heaved that rock at Aunt Gertrude. Or maybe they'll squirt us with nerve gas as they pass."

Joe spoke over his shoulder to Ira Gort. "Are those gas pens given to all members of HAVOC?"

Gort nodded anxiously. "Most of their agents have one. And that gas is really effective. One noseful and we'd all be writhing in misery for about ten seconds—then we'd pass out, and your car would go out of control!"

"Then keep your window up, Frank!" Joe said to his brother.

"You, too! Those creeps are liable to pass us on either side, whichever chance comes first!" As Frank's eyes darted to the rearview mirror again, he broke into a sudden smile. "Here comes the U. S. Cavalry!"

Biff Hooper's rainbow-streaked van was roaring up behind them in the lefthand lane! Frank let it draw abreast long enough to exchange hasty signals with Biff. A moment later, the Hardys' engine changed from a mellow purr to a deepthroated blast. The yellow sports car shot ahead and, before the maroon sedan could increase speed to give chase, the van nosed in between them.

Another wave of traffic was surging toward them from the rear. Biff veered from side to side to keep their enemies from passing, despite its occupants' furious looks and loud horn blasts. At the same time, he slowed the van's speed to give the oncoming traffic time to engulf them. Soon they were both hemmed in by a steady stream of cars and trucks on either side. The HAVOC gangsters were neatly clamped in the jaws of a fast-moving trap!

Joe chuckled as the Hardys' sports car left their pursuers far behind. "Good old Biff!"

Frank turned off the expressway at the nearest exit. After weaving a zigzag course through a number of side roads, he finally resumed their homeward trip to Bayport. Instead of entering town, however, he skirted around the seaside community and turned onto the highway that led westward through the hills. At last, he stopped outside the Burton O. Bradley Company building, which housed the Bureau of Bombs.

"Great work, boys!" John Smith congratulated the Hardys as they brought Ira Gort into the agency chief's office. "So this is Igor, eh?"

He invited them all to sit down, then went on, "The process of fully debriefing an enemy agent may take weeks, of course, or even months. But suppose we start with a few questions and answers right now."

Frank and Joe noticed that Gort's manner had changed. Now that they had reached BOB safely, he no longer seemed nervous and fearful. His face had regained its normal, hard-jawed look, and his manner was not only confident, but even cocky and sly.

"Not so fast, Smith," Gort told the agency chief. "You're forgetting something, aren't you?"

"What's that?"

"Before I do any talking, the agreement was that I'd be paid off with a million-dollar emerald."

"You'd have had it by now," Smith replied, "but the gem was stolen yesterday from a bonded messenger of the Winfield Jewelry Company. We'll work out something, but in the meantime that needn't stop us from getting some key facts right now, such as the name and whereabouts of HAV-OC's local boss of operations in this country. Time may be precious!"

"Then don't waste it!" The stocky gangster with his closely-cropped, silver-blond hair grinned coldly at the agency chief. "Pay me the emerald that I was promised, and I'll tell you whatever you want to know. Until then, you'll get no information out of me."

Smith eyed Gort coldly. "You know it isn't easy to purchase an emerald worth a million dollars. Even with luck, it could take us another forty-eight hours to lay hands on a stone that big."

"Then you'd better start looking hard and fast!"

Both Frank and Joe had been turning the case over and over in their minds ever since Frank's hunch about the identity of Igor had proved correct. The same thoughts were passing through both their heads at this moment as they exchanged significant glances.

But this time it was the younger Hardy boy who spoke up. "Excuse me, sir—do you mind if I use your phone?"

Smith looked surprised but gestured to the instrument on his desk. "Go right ahead."

After checking with directory assistance to get Jasper Hunt's telephone listing in Axton, Joe dialed the number. Orva Danner answered.

"Mrs. Danner," he said, "when you phoned Gort Security to have a guard meet your brother at the airport, did you by any chance tell Mr. Gort the name of the hotel where your brother was staying in Colombia?"

Mrs. Danner took a moment to reflect before replying. "Why, yes, I believe I did, now that you ask. Let me think back . . . Yes, I know I did. Mr. Gort asked me a number of questions, you see. Like whether the guard should wear plain clothes and remain undercover or be in uniform and identify himself openly as soon as my brother landed. Things like that. I wasn't too sure myself, so Mr. Gort suggested that it might be simpler if he talked to my brother directly to clear up these questions. So I told him the name of the hotel and let him call Bogotá himself."

"Thanks a lot, Mrs. Danner. I'll explain later why I wanted to know." After hanging up, Joe flashed a triumphant look at his brother. "I'll bet we can both guess who stole that emerald—right, Frank?"

Gort's face remained impassive, but John Smith frowned at the two young sleuths. "What's all this?"

Joe reported what Sam Radley had found out at the Mirador Hotel in Bogotá. Then he went on, "Gort could have arranged for a South American HAVOC agent to go there and inject Jasper Hunt with a drug just before Hunt checked out."

"Why?" Smith asked.

"Because he'd just learned from Mrs. Danner that her brother was bringing back something valuable—so valuable, in fact, that he wanted a guard on hand to protect him once he arrived in New York. We think that valuable item was a huge emerald worth a million dollars."

"Once Hunt was drugged," Frank put in, "the HAVOC agent could have given him post-hypnotic instructions to go to that particular address in Manhattan where he was ambushed and robbed— probably by American thugs working for HAVOC."

"When Gort learned the loot was an emerald," Joe went on, "that could be what gave him the idea of asking for a million-dollar emerald as his price for defecting."

"Being in the security business," Frank said, "he probably knows all about the bonded messengers used to deliver gems. Through his business contacts, or maybe from his personal acquaintances, he could have found out when the gem designated for Igor was being delivered to Bayport."

"So he shadowed the messenger and swiped the stone," Joe ended. "A neat way to make himself an extra million bucks, because he expected BOB to come up with another emerald of the same size."

While the Hardys were speaking, Gort's expression had changed from a sneer to a look of angry exasperation. "You're both nuts!" he exclaimed. "I don't know anything about that jewelry messenger you're talking about. Go ahead—just try and prove your crazy theory!"

"They won't have to," Smith snapped. "We'll settle the question here and now!"

He issued a brusque order over his desk intercom. A moment later, two armed guards walked in.

Smith gestured towards Gort. "Search him."

The brawny guards seized Gort by the arms, jerked him out of his chair, and proceeded to frisk him despite his heated protests.

"Satisfied now?" he growled when the search was completed, glaring first at the Hardys, then at John Smith.

"Maybe and maybe not." No emerald had been

found on Gort's person, but Smith extracted a small key from a zippered pocket of the prisoner's wallet. "What's this for?"

"The mailbox of my apartment."

"You don't say?" The agency chief smiled after studying the key for several moments. "It happens this key was designed for a high-security lock—a kind used for strongboxes and also by banks. In case you didn't know it, Gort, the FBI has developed quite a data file on keys. Let's see what they can tell us about this one. It even has a serial number on it, not to mention the manufacturer's insignia."

Smith excused himself long enough to have the key photocopied and the resulting picture transmitted over the agency's computer link to the FBI in Washington.

Within moments, the answer flashed on the screen of Smith's computer terminal.

"Your mailbox, eh?" There was an icy grin on the agency chief's face as he glanced contemptuously at Gort. "According to the FBI, this is a key to safe-deposit box number 257 at the Adams Bank & Trust Company in Newark, New Jersey."

Gort flushed but remained stonily silent.

"There's one way to find out for sure what's in that safe-deposit box," Frank volunteered. "If you're willing to trust us, Joe and I will drive there right now and bring back the contents."

"Good idea!" Smith handed Frank the key. "You boys get going. I'll call the New Jersey State Police and have them arrange for you to be admitted to the bank's vault."

The Hardys hurried out to their car.

"If the turnpike's not too crowded," Frank said, "we should be able to make it there and back in—"

"What's the matter?" Joe queried. He had already opened the passenger-side door of their yellow sports car and was about to climb in when he noticed that his brother had paused and was staring suspiciously at the front end.

"The hood's not latched tight," Frank said in a tense voice.

"What do you mean?"

"I mean it was shut tight when we went inside the building!" Frank's face had suddenly taken on a look of frantic anxiety. "Joe, I think the car's been tampered with! Come on! Get away from it as fast as you can!"

As he spoke, Frank took off at a sprint. Joe did likewise. In his nervous haste, Joe gave the door a careless shove with one hand to close it as he darted back toward the building.

It slammed shut an instant later. There was a loud *boom!* as the fuel tank exploded. The whole car was suddenly engulfed in an orange ball of flames!

20 *Rattlesnake Roundup*

The Hardys had been hurled to the ground by the blast but were otherwise unharmed. As they picked themselves up, they felt the searing wave of heat from their car. It was now the center of a blazing inferno, which would soon leave their beloved yellow sports sedan a blackened metal hulk!

"Come on!" Frank urged. "We'd better get back inside the building!"

"Wh-what happened?" Joe asked, still a bit dazed.

"Our car was most probably wired to explode when one of us turned the key in the ignition," Frank explained. "When you slammed the door, that jar alone must have been enough to set off the detonator."

Shocked by the sudden fiery disaster, Joe was inclined to linger and stare at the glowing cocoon of flame while he collected his wits. But Frank grabbed him by the arm and hurried him inside.

The agency was in an uproar. Personnel who had heard or glimpsed the explosion through their windows were crowding into the lobby. Most of them would have rushed outside for a better view of the fire had Frank not urged the agency chief to hold them back.

"The bomb must have been planted after Joe and I arrived," he said hastily. "That means we were tailed here even though we thought we'd shaken off our pursuers. Or maybe they just guessed that this is where we'd bring Igor. There could be HAVOC agents out there right now, keeping watch on this place from the woods!"

John Smith frowned. "Are you implying that anyone who steps outside might be in danger?"

Frank shrugged anxiously. "No telling what they've got in mind, sir. They probably want to snatch Igor before he spills enough to put the whole gang behind bars. They might try to take hostages to bargain with—or maybe shoot anyone who attempts to leave, just to show they mean business. If there are enough of them, they might even risk an armed assault on the building!"

Suddenly, the telephone on the lobby desk rang shrilly. The receptionist guard answered, then shot a startled glance at the agency chief. "It's HAVOC calling, sir!"

Smith took the phone. "Who is this?" he demanded sharply. A tense conversation followed. The lobby lights dimmed out while he spoke. Smith's face was grim as he hung up several minutes later. "You're right, Frank—they've got the building surrounded. They tapped our phone line to make that call. Otherwise they've cut off all our connections with the outside world—power lines, phone lines, computer cable, you name it."

There were gasps of dismay as the Hardys stared back at the speaker.

"Then we're isolated here," Frank said.

"Totally. Not only that, they've been putting in mines during the last twenty minutes. The caller claimed that bombs have been planted all around the perimeter of the building—enough explosives to demolish the structure and cause a cave-in of our subterranean chambers. He's given us exactly ten minutes to surrender before they set off the charges!"

"What happens if we all just rush out right now?" Joe asked.

"Detonation will occur immediately!"

192

A stunned silence greeted the agency chief's report. But it lasted for only seconds before Smith's aides began to offer suggestions on how to cope with the crisis. A hasty council of war ensued.

BOB was well-equipped with bomb-detection gear, and the building complex had several secret exits. It was therefore suggested that detection teams might slip out to locate and disarm the explosive charges. But could they do so unseen and finish the job before the deadline was up and the HAVOC agents detonated the bombs?

"Maybe my brother and I can gain a little extra time for you," Frank spoke up suddenly.

"How?" Smith asked.

"By walking right out the front door and signaling that we want to speak to them. Perhaps we can divert their attention and keep them talking long enough for your men to defuse the bombs."

Smith was unwilling to risk the boys' safety. But Joe abruptly cut short his protests. "Come on, Frank—let's give it a try!"

Before the agency chief or anyone else could stop them, the Hardys were striding out the door. With their hands up and waving white handkerchiefs, they waited for the HAVOC agents to show themselves.

Presently an armed and uniformed figure stepped

out into view from among the trees that bordered the grounds of the Burton O. Bradley building. Frank and Joe recognized him as the chauffeur of the maroon sedan.

"This way!" he shouted. "And no tricks!"

He prodded the boys ahead of him toward a small clearing, where four more men stood waiting. One was easily recognizable as the crook who had disguised himself as an old lady. The Hardys guessed that two more—one with a drooping, dark mustache, the other a thickset, tough-looking individual —were probably the frogman and his accomplice who had harassed them at Bayview Beach.

But it was the fourth man, a burly, masked figure, who dominated the scene. From the way he promptly took charge of the conversation, he was obviously their leader—the boss of HAVOC's North American operations.

"No doubt you've recognized the driver of that maroon sedan," he said to the boys with a sinister chuckle. "I'm afraid your efforts to dodge us were a complete waste of time."

"How come?" Joe asked.

"Because an electronic bug was attached to your car after you left it in that open-air lot near Central Park!" He chuckled again as he saw the disgusted expression on the Hardys' faces. "Actually, you were trailed all the way from Bayport to New York, you see. Of course, once you'd picked up Gort, we wanted you to *think* you'd given us the slip in order to throw you and BOB off guard."

"Maybe you've got a surprise coming, too," Frank retorted defiantly, "if you think the five of you have any chance of seizing control of BOB!"

"A clever remark, my boy," the HAVOC leader responded. "What you're really trying to find out is the number of men under my command. Let me merely assure you that I have numerous HAVOC agents watching the building all around."

Both Frank and Joe felt a twinge of despair. If the building were indeed being watched on all sides, the bomb-detection teams had little chance of success. Before they could find and defuse the explosive charges, they would probably be picked off by HAVOC snipers.

"I suggest you come to the point quickly," the masked man went on, his voice suddenly turning harsh. "What is it you Hardys wish to talk to me about? Or are you merely stalling for time?" His tone had now taken on a definite note of menace.

The two boys knew they must act fast or their mission was hopeless. Joe's eyes widened in a sudden look of speechless terror.

"Snap out of it!" the HAVOC boss rasped. "If

195

you've nothing more to say, you'll both get what's coming to you right now!"

"Th-that rattlesnake!" Joe exclaimed, pointing to their feet. "Gas it, Frank!"

His words caught their captors completely by surprise. Had he spoken or pointed without putting on such a good act, they would no doubt have suspected a trick. As it was, their gaze followed his finger almost involuntarily. Instantly, Joe whirled and kicked the weapon from the chauffeur's hands.

Frank was already whipping out the gas pen that he had snatched away from the fake old lady. The pen was barely out of his jacket pocket, however, when the mustached crook seized his wrist and tried to make him drop it.

Joe, meanwhile, dove to the ground. Clawing up handfuls of sandy soil, he flung it in the other crooks' eyes. Before they could recover from their temporary blindness, he hurled himself at them, punching and kicking. Frank had landed a hard blow in the mustached crook's stomach that left him gasping for breath.

In moments, the Hardy boys and the five HAVOC gangsters were in a tangled, furious melee. Frank and Joe purposely fought back to back, knowing that such close-quarters combat would cause their enemies to get in each other's way and thus prevent them from bringing their full force to bear on the two youths.

Their struggles, however, would probably have been hopeless had a car not suddenly pulled up on the bureau grounds with a squeal of brakes. Two men leaped out and ran through the trees to the boys' assistance. One was a tall, broad-shouldered man in his forties. The other was not quite as big, but fast-moving and hard-fisted.

Frank was the first to recognize them. "It's Dad, Joe!" he cried out to his brother. "And Sam Radley!"

Even though still outnumbered, the Hardys and Sam Radley were more than a match for their opponents. The fight would soon have been over, but the HAVOC boss managed to pull a small walkie-talkie from his pocket to summon his other thugs who were posted about the building.

Half-a-dozen gangsters came running to answer their leader's call for help. By this time, however, Smith and his aides in the building had glimpsed what was going on outside. Even though the explosive charges had not yet been found and defused, BOB agents rushed out to join in the fray. Within five minutes, the entire subversive group had been rounded up and taken prisoners.

John Smith reached out to snatch off their boss' mask. But the Hardy boys had already identified him by his voice.

"His name's George Gamma," said Frank. "His front is an outfit called Gamma Importers. That's the firm that sold the emerald to Winfield Jewelry."

The crook's jowly face twisted in a snarl. "I should have taken care of you punks when you first showed up in my office!"

"That'll be enough out of you!" Smith snapped, then gestured to two of the agency guards. "Take him away."

"How did you get here, Dad?" Joe asked joyfully as Fenton Hardy embraced his two sons.

"Sam and I made contact in Bogotá and flew home by military jet," the ace detective replied. "And it looks like we got here just in time!"

Before the afternoon was over, it was learned that the missing emerald was indeed in Gort's safe-deposit box at the Newark bank. Gort confessed to stealing the gem from the bonded messenger in hopes of doubling his profit for defecting. He was now eager to cooperate and tell all he knew about HAVOC's North American operations in order to save himself from going to prison for the robbery. But his crime had cost him any chance of collecting a million-dollar fee as a paid informant.

At dinner that evening, Joe suddenly thought of the man whose disappearance had brought the Hardy boys into the exciting case. "I wonder if Jasper Hunt's out of his coma," he remarked.

"You'll soon see for yourself," Aunt Gertrude remarked. Her eyes twinkled behind her gold-rimmed glasses as she added, "Mrs. Danner called just before you got home. Her brother was released from the hospital today. They're going to stop by on their way home in order to thank you fellows in person."

Their red-bearded visitor arrived with his sister a half-hour later, and Frank and Joe finally heard the whole story from his own lips.

Jasper Hunt had found the huge emerald while hiking through the mountains of Colombia. The HAVOC gang, however, had got wind of his find from local Indians. They planned to rob Hunt. But Fenton Hardy, who was already on the gang's trail, learned of the caper and rescued his fellow American. Then, to ensure his safety, he escorted Hunt partway to Bogotá.

Meanwhile, Igor had been in touch with Mr. Hardy to hint at his willingness to defect from the gang even before the famed sleuth had gone to South America. Later he had managed to send him a secret radio message. As a result, Mr. Hardy had jotted down the name and address of Gort Security. Jasper Hunt happened to see the notation while he was with the detective in Colombia. He wrongly assumed that the firm was a reliable security outfit, which the detective sometimes called on to aid his own investigations. As a result, he suggested that his sister call Gort Security to provide an armed guard when he landed at Kennedy Airport with his emerald.

Gort, as a member of the HAVOC gang, already knew that Hunt's valuable item was a huge gem. So he arranged with Mr. Gamma to have it stolen by means of the drug injection administered to Hunt at the hotel in Bogotá before takeoff, and the rooming house ambush in New York after his return to this country.

Knowing that Gamma Importers had immediately sold the gem to Winfield Jewelry, a client of Fenton Hardy's, Gort then cunningly asked for a million-dollar emerald as his price for defection. The earlier-dated bill of sale and import clearance that Gamma showed the Hardy boys had, of course, been faked.

Frank and Joe slept late the following morning, recovering from their arduous efforts in rounding up the HAVOC gang. When they awoke, Frank yawned, then said, "We're out of work, Joe!"

Joe nodded glumly. "Maybe we'll get another case soon."

They would, and it was called *Trapped at Sea*.

The boys were just about to get up when their father strode into their room with unexpected news.

"I forgot to tell you fellows that Winfield Jewelry called yesterday afternoon," the detective announced. "They want to show their appreciation for the way you two helped to recover their stolen emerald. So they sent over a small reward. It just arrived."

"What is it, Dad?" Joe asked eagerly. "Did you open it yet?"

Mr. Hardy's lips twitched in a faint smile. "Not exactly. But they asked me for suggestions, so I happen to know what it is."

"Well? What is it?" Frank chimed in.

"Better go see for yourselves!"

The boys hurried downstairs, then looked around questioningly at their father. He merely smiled and pointed out the window.

Frank and Joe looked, gasped, and dashed out the front door, forgetting they were clad only in pajamas and bathrobes.

Standing in the driveway was a gleaming, brand-new model of their beloved yellow sports sedan!

THE HARDY BOYS® SERIES
by Franklin W. Dixon

You will also enjoy

THE TOM SWIFT® SERIES
by Victor Appleton